HELP!
I'M TRAPPED IN
MY SISTER'S BODY

Other Books by Todd Strasser

Help! I'm Trapped in the President's Body

Help! I'm Trapped in My Gym Teacher's Body

Howl-A-Ween

Help! I'm Trapped in Obedience School

Abe Lincoln for Class President

Help! I'm Trapped in the First Day of School

Please Don't Be Mine, Julie Valentine

Help! I'm Trapped in My Teacher's Body

The Diving Bell

Free Willy (novelization)

Jumanji™ (novelization)

Home Alone™ (novelization)

Home Alone™ *II: Lost in New York* (novelization)

The Mall From Outer Space

HELP!
I'M TRAPPED IN
MY SISTER'S BODY

TODD STRASSER

AN
APPLE
PAPERBACK

SCHOLASTIC INC.
New York Toronto London Auckland Sydney

to Sara and Ben Zuckert

No part of this publication may be reproduced in whole or in part, or stored in a retrieval system, or transmitted in any form or by any means, electronic, mechanical, photocopying, recording, or otherwise, without written permission of the publisher. For information regarding permission, write to Scholastic Inc., 555 Broadway, New York, NY 10012.

ISBN 0-590-92167-3

12 11 10 9 8 7 6 5 4 3 2 1   7 8 9/9 0 1 2/0

Printed in the U.S.A.   40

First Scholastic printing, January 1997

HELP!
I'M TRAPPED IN
MY SISTER'S BODY

1

"Your sister's armpits smell *so* bad, the teacher gave her an A for *not* raising her hand," Andy said.

Andy, Josh, and I were out on the street in front of my house, throwing a football around. Andy and I were wearing white T-shirts and navy sweatpants. Josh was wearing a gray sweatshirt and jeans.

"Oh, yeah?" I said. "Well, your brother's so dumb he sold his car for gas money."

"Yeah?" said Andy. "Well, your sister's been in the same grade for so long everyone thinks she's the teacher."

"Yeah?" I shot back. "Well, your brother's so stupid he sat on the TV and watched the *couch*."

"Oh, yeah?" Andy said. "Well — "

"*Will you guys shut up!*" Josh shouted. "All you do is diss each other. I'm sick of it. Let's play ball. I'm going out for a pass, Jake. See if you can hit me."

Josh started to jog away. I pulled the football back and heaved, but my throw was short and bounced on the street behind him.

"Your aim is so bad you could throw at the ground and miss," Andy quipped.

"Oh, yeah?" I sputtered. "Well, you're so uncoordinated you slept on the floor and *still* fell out of bed!"

"Oh, yeah?" Andy began. "Well — "

"*Shut up!*" Josh screamed at both of us. His face was red. "You want to know how dumb both of *you* are? You spent all afternoon dissing each other when you could have been working on plays for the big game tomorrow."

He handed the football to Andy, then turned to me. "For the last time, Jake, let's try to practice something. We'll do a crossing pattern. We both go straight out, count to three and cross. Got it?"

I nodded.

"Okay, *hike!*" Andy yelled.

I took off down the street. At the count of three I cut left and looked back. Andy had released a perfect spiral right toward me. All I had to do was —

Oof! The football slid through my fingers and fell to the street. Another mess up. As I ran after the ball, I heard someone chuckle.

"Great catch, Jake." It was my sister, Jessica, rubbing it in as usual.

I straightened up. She looked different. Her

long straight brown hair was now curly. It had a reddish tint when the sunlight fell on it. She was wearing a tight red sweater and a short skirt. A strange scent filled the air around her.

"What happened to *you*?" I asked.

Jessica touched her new hair self-consciously. "What do you mean?"

"I mean it's not Halloween, so what's with the costume?"

Jessica narrowed her eyes angrily. She reached down and picked up the football. "Go out for a long one, Andy."

Andy started to run. Jessica held the ball and waited. Andy kept running down the street away from us.

"Forget it," I said. "There's *no way* you can throw that far."

A second later Jessica heaved a perfect bomb.

"*Amazing!*" Josh gasped as the ball sailed high into the air.

Andy stretched his arms out and just managed to snag the pass. He started jogging back to us. "Great throw, Jessica."

Jessica gave me one of her superior looks.

"You got lucky," I said.

"Oh?" Her eyebrows rose and she glowered at me. Then she turned to Andy. "I'm going to run a slant pattern, down and out. Think you can hit me?"

"I'll try," Andy said.

Jessica took off down the street with her new hair bouncing and her short skirt flapping. Andy heaved the football. Too high! It was going to fly over her head.

"Bad pass." Andy shook his head. "My fault."

But as the ball sailed over her, Jessica stretched way up and grabbed it with her fingertips.

"*Unreal!*" Josh cried. He and Andy gave me funny looks. I knew what they were thinking: *Too bad I was playing in the big game tomorrow, and not Jessica.*

2

"Thanks for making me look like a total wuss in front of my friends," I said later when Jessica and I were in the kitchen eating spaghetti for dinner.

"You deserved it," Jessica shot back. "For making that crack about my hair."

"I only said that because *you* made that crack about me missing the football," I said. "*You're* the one who started it. And you didn't have to make me look bad in public."

"Oh?" she frowned. "What was I *supposed* to do?"

"Wait until we're alone," I said. "You can humiliate me all you want. Just do it in private."

"I'll be sure to remember that next time." She rolled her eyes.

"You just don't get it," I said, gnawing angrily on my thumbnail. "The *worst* thing you can do is make a guy look bad in sports."

"Come off it, Jake," my sister replied, like she didn't believe me. "It's only sports."

"*Only* sports?" I gasped. "Are you crazy? Sports is *everything* when you're fourteen. There's hardly anything else that even *matters*."

Jessica gazed up at the ceiling and let out a big sigh. "You're totally hopeless."

"*I'm* hopeless?" I shot back. "Look who's talking. I bet you paid a fortune to make your hair kinky, red, and *ugly*. You spend half your life in your room putting on makeup and taking it off, and trying on outfit after outfit. Didn't anyone ever tell you they're *only* clothes?"

My sister looked down her nose at me. "You don't understand anything, Jake."

"Wrong. I understand *lots* of things. The only thing I don't understand is *you*!" Once again that weird scent wafted into my nose.

"And what's that smell anyway?" I asked.

"What smell?"

"The smell I smell every time you get close."

Jessica bit her lip and tugged nervously at her earlobe. "You don't like it?"

"Get real, Jess. It smells like roadkill that's been left in the sun too long."

Jessica's jaw tightened. Her eyes began to get watery, but she blinked back the tears. She stood up. "You are the meanest, cruelest little bratty excuse for a human being I've ever seen. I'm glad I made you look like a wuss in front of your friends, because you *are* a wuss, Jake. You can't throw, you can't catch. The only thing worse than you on a football field would be a corpse."

She stomped out of the kitchen, slamming the door closed behind her.

3

I finished dinner and went up to my room. Across the hall I could hear Jessica in her room gabbing on her phone as usual. I felt bad because of what she'd said, *and* because of what I'd said. Maybe she was right. Maybe I had been mean to her.

But she'd been mean to me.

And she'd started it.

Yeah, yeah, I know two wrongs don't make a right.

But why do I have to be the first to admit it?

I was just about to go into my room when I heard the phone ring in my parents' room. I knew Jessica wouldn't answer it because she was on her own line, so I answered it.

"Hello?"

"Hey, Jake." It was my dad. From the sound of it, he was calling from the car.

"Hi, Dad, what's up?"

"Your mom and I are stuck in traffic. I think

we're going to be here a while. Have you had dinner?"

"Yeah, Jessica made spaghetti."

"Good," Dad said. "Listen, there's something I forgot to tell you. Mr. Hoshino is coming by tomorrow with his daughter Sumiko."

"Wha ... ?" I felt my jaw drop in surprise.

"They're over here from Tokyo. Mr. Hoshino and I have some business to discuss. Think you could show Sumiko around for the day?"

"Uh ... I ... I guess," I stammered.

"Great. We'll see you later." He hung up.

In a daze I stumbled into my room and sat on my bed. Sumiko Hoshino was coming *here?* For the past year she and I had been trading E-mail over the Internet. Our dads did business together. It was my dad's idea that I become pen pals with her. Except for him, I'd never told anyone about her.

Rap! Rap! A knock on my door shook me out of my dazed state.

"What do you want?" I yelled.

The door opened and Jessica stuck her head in. "Got a second?"

"For you? No."

She came in anyway and stood just inside the door, where she crossed her arms and gave me an earnest look. "Why do we have to be so mean to each other?"

I could have made some cruel, snappy, nasty

reply, but I was getting tired of that. So I said, "I don't know, Jess. Maybe that's just the way brothers and sisters are supposed to be."

"All we do is hurt each other's feelings," Jessica pointed out. "I mean, maybe we should try to understand each other more."

"You want the totally honest truth?" I said. "Even if I tried for the next *thousand* years I'd never understand what it's like to be you."

"Why not?" my sister asked.

"Because I don't break down in tears when I can't decide what to wear. I don't throw a fit when my makeup isn't right, or when I don't like my hair. You, on the other hand, do that at least once a week."

Jessica thought about it for a moment. "You're right, Jake. You can't understand what it's like to be me. So how about this? Even though we don't understand each other, let's at least try to be nice to each other, okay?"

She came over and held out her hand.

I stared at her. "I just want to remind you that you're the one who started the whole thing in the first place by making fun of me in front of my friends."

I expected her to argue, but to my surprise, she nodded in agreement. "I know, but I'm supposed to see Dr. Paine tomorrow morning. He has to fill three cavities and they're *deep*."

"So?" I asked.

"You know how edgy I get when I have to see the dentist," she explained.

"I don't know what the big deal is," I said. "All he has to do is shoot you up with Novocain and you won't feel a thing."

My sister turned pale. That's when I remembered that the one thing she hates even more than the dentist is getting a shot.

"Let's not talk about it," she said, still holding out her hand. "Let's just agree not to be so mean to each other from now on, okay?"

"Okay." I shook her hand. Once again that weird scent wafted into my nose. "What *is* that smell?"

"Patchouli oil," Jessica said. "It smells a little strange at first, but you get used to it."

"You mean, you *wear* it?"

"Yes."

"What's the point?" I asked.

"I just don't want to be like every other girl, that's all."

"I don't think that's something you have to worry about," I replied.

Jessica stiffened. "I thought we just agreed to be nice to each other."

"You're right," I admitted. "Let's pretend I meant it in a nice way."

Jessica nodded and left my room. In a way, I

was kind of relieved that we'd agreed not to pick on each other anymore. It made life nicer.

In the meantime, my thoughts turned back to Sumiko Hoshino.

She was coming to visit tomorrow.

Suddenly I had a major problem.

4

"You want *me* to switch bodies with *you*?" Jessica looked up from her homework and stared at me in disbelief.

"Just for tomorrow morning," I said.

"Forget it." She turned back to her books.

"I thought we were going to be nice to each other from now on," I reminded her.

"That's right," Jessica said without looking up. "But switching bodies with you goes *way beyond* being nice."

"Why?" I asked.

For a second Jessica looked like she was going to say something mean, but then she swallowed her tongue. "Let's just drop it, okay?"

"If we switch, you won't have to go to the dentist," I said. "I'll go for you."

The creases between my sister's eyes deepened. I could tell that she was actually considering it. "And what would I have to do for you?"

"Uh . . . play touch football?"

Jessica eyed me suspiciously. "There has to be more to this, Jake. There's something you're not telling me."

There was something. Or *someone*. The last thing I wanted to do was tell her about Sumiko. Jessica would probably goof on me for the next three trillion years. But it looked like I had no choice.

"Just remember, it was your idea that we should be nice to each other from now on," I said to prepare her.

Jessica nodded, but I saw a twinkle in her eye. She knew something good was coming.

"Well, there's this girl," I started. "From Japan." Then I went on to tell her the whole story of how Sumi was coming to visit with her father.

"Aw, isn't that cute?" Jessica grinned. "Little Jakey-poo's got a secret girlfriend."

"I thought you agreed to be nice," I reminded her.

"Saying you have a secret girlfriend isn't being mean," Jessica said. "I think it's sweet."

I gave her a suspicious look. I wasn't sure I believed her. "Well, she's not my girlfriend anyway. She's just a pen pal."

"Then what's the problem?" Jessica asked.

"Well, uh, you see, I, er, well, I told her something that isn't exactly, er, true." My face was growing hot with embarrassment.

14

Jessica's eyes seemed to sparkle with delight. "What?"

"Swear you won't tell anyone?" I asked.

"Yes."

"Cross your heart?"

"Yes."

Then I noticed her hands were hidden under her desk. "You're not crossing your fingers, are you?"

"No."

"Show me."

"For Pete's sake." Jessica showed me her hands. "I promise I won't tell anyone."

"Okay." I took a deep breath. "I told Sumi . . . that I was a really good athlete."

"*Ha! Ha!*" Jessica burst into laughter.

"I thought we agreed to be nice," I grumbled.

"Okay, okay. Just let me catch my breath." Jessica stopped laughing, but she still had a big grin on her face. "Of all the things to tell her, Jake. Didn't you ever learn that it doesn't pay to fib?"

"But she lives *on the other side of the world,*" I said, exasperated. "How was I supposed to know she'd come here?"

"So just tell her the truth," Jessica said.

I shook my head.

"Why not?" she asked.

I pressed my lips together and said nothing.

My sister furrowed her brow. Then the smile grew bigger. "Oh, I get it," she said. "She's just a pen pal *now*, but you're hoping that maybe, if you play your cards right, she could be more."

If my face felt hot before, it was on fire now. "If you make fun of me, so help me I'll — "

"Take a chill pill, Jake." Jessica calmly crossed her arms. "Besides, it won't work. We can't switch bodies anyway. Tomorrow's Saturday and school's closed. We couldn't get in to use Mr. Dirksen's machine even if we wanted to."

"Wrong. School's open from eight until noon for a young writers' conference," I informed her.

My sister picked up a pencil and tapped it against her textbook. It looked like she was still thinking about it. But then she shook her head.

"I can't, Jake."

"Why not?"

"I just can't."

Now it was my turn to eye her suspiciously. "I think there's something *you're* not telling *me.*"

"You're right." Jessica turned back to her homework.

"So tell me."

"No."

"Why not? I told you my secret, didn't I?"

"There's no rule that says just because you do something I have to do it too."

She was right, but it annoyed me anyway. "So tomorrow, instead of playing touch football, you'd rather be sitting in Dr. Paine's dentist's chair?"

16

Jessica didn't look up from her homework. "That's right, Jake."

"*Eeeeeeeeiiiiiiinnnnnnnnnnnne!*" I made the sound of a dentist's drill.

"Stop it, Jake."

"*Eeeeeeeeiiiiiiinnnnnnnnnnnne!*"

"I thought we agreed to be nice to each other," she said.

"Just because I'm imitating a dentist's drill doesn't mean I'm not being nice," I said. "*Eeeeeeeeiiiiiiinnnnnnnnnnnne!*"

"Well, it doesn't sound nice to me."

"Okay, I'll make a different sound. *Ahhhhhhhhhhhhh!*" I screamed as if I was being tortured. "*Look out! Here comes the Novocain!*"

Whap! Jessica slammed her pen down on her desk and shouted, "*Get out!*"

I backed toward the door. "Come on, Jessica, why not switch with me? You know you can't stand the idea of going to Dr. Paine's. You play football for me and I'll get drilled for you. It'll be perfect."

Brrrrriiiinnnngggg! The phone next to Jessica's bed rang. She has her own phone because if she isn't putting on makeup, trying on outfits, or doing her homework, she's usually gabbing away with one of her friends. She answered it. "Hello? Oh, hi, Dan."

"*Winters?*" I whispered. Dan "Zitface" Winters

was a tenth-grader who thought he was Mr. Totally Suave.

"Could you hold on a second, Dan?" Jessica
clamped her hands around the receiver and
hissed at me. *"Get out, or I'll kill you!"*

"Tsk, tsk." I wagged a finger at her. "I thought
we were going to be nice."

Jessica shot daggers at me with her eyes. I left
her room, but stopped outside the door and listened.

"Nothing, Dan, just my annoying little
brother," Jessica said. "Two o'clock sounds fine.
Great, see you tomorrow."

*So that was why Jessica didn't want to switch
bodies with me!* She had a date!

5

As soon as my sister was off the phone I pushed open her door and went back in. "Why would you go *anywhere* with that jerk?" I asked. "You know he chases every girl he sees."

Jessica looked surprised. "You listened?"

"Hey." I shrugged. "That's what annoying little brothers do, right?"

My sister sighed and shook her head. "I can't believe I promised to be nice to you."

"So." I rubbed my chin. "Tomorrow at two o'clock. Wonder what *that's* all about? Hey, I know! He's taking you to the carnival!"

Jessica smirked. "You're so smart, Jake."

"But why should that stop you from switching with me in the morning?" I asked.

"I just don't want to take any chances," she replied.

"Chances? You mean you're worried that something will go wrong and you won't get to be with Zitface?"

"Would you please stop calling him that?" Jessica asked. "His name happens to be Dan."

"Dan Winters . . . " I shook my head in amazement. "I thought you had taste. Guess I was wrong."

"So much for being nice to each other," my sister said wistfully.

"Okay, look, I'll be nice," I said. "I just want to know one thing. And this is serious. Why *him*? I mean, let's forget for a second that he's got more holes in his face than the dark side of the moon. The guy's a scuzzball."

"You're so typical, Jake," Jessica replied. "I mean, could you be a little less jealous?"

"*Jealous?* No way. I'd just really like to know what girls see in him."

"Well, he's the only boy in my grade who acts mature," my sister said. "He's very self-assured and he isn't afraid to treat a girl nicely. And even though he does have a *minor* skin problem, he's still one of the better-looking boys, and a very good dresser."

"Know what we just learned in school?" I said. "In the old days, guess what they called guys who dressed real fancy?"

"I don't know," my sister said. "What?"

"Dandies," I said. "Dandy Dan the Zitface Man."

Jessica made a face. "That's really brilliant, Jake."

Then I had an idea. "Hey, if you have a date with Dandy Dan tomorrow, it's even more important that you and I switch. Otherwise you're going to be up all night worrying about Dr. Paine. You'll miss your beauty sleep. Tomorrow you'll probably have big dark ugly rings under your eyes. I bet Dandy Dan won't find that very attractive. And your hair won't get any sleep either. Ever heard of tired limp hair? That's what you're going to have tomorrow. And — "

"Good try, Jake." Jessica waved good-bye. "Now be nice and . . . disappear."

6

That night I lay in bed, gnawing on my finger-nails. I had a serious problem. For almost a year I'd been trading E-mail with Sumi, and I hadn't exactly been honest. Most of my lies had been in the area of athletics. I'd kind of hinted that I was a really good athlete. Actually, I'd pretty much said I was so good that I was being scouted by a bunch of major professional teams.

The truth is that no eighth-grader in history has ever been scouted by a major professional team.

But as long as Sumi was halfway around the world, it didn't matter, right?

I glanced at the clock on the nightstand: 10 P.M. In about twelve hours Sumi was going to arrive. Just in time for the big touch football game. It wouldn't take her long to figure out that I wasn't the greatest athlete around.

Rap! Rap! Someone knocked on my door.

"Yeah?" I called.

"It's me." Jessica pushed the door open.

We stared at each other in the dim light. She hardly ever came to my room. Now she'd come twice in the same day. It had to be some kind of record.

"What's up?" I asked.

Jessica tugged on her earlobe. "First thing in the morning, you have to take a long shower and change into all clean clothes."

"Serious?" I gasped.

She nodded.

"How come you changed your mind?"

"Dr. Paine."

"Can't stand the thought of that torture, huh?" I had to smile to myself.

"Let's not talk about it," Jessica said. "Just make sure you wash *everywhere.*"

"Deal." I couldn't believe she was going to do it!

Jessica sighed. "I must be crazy."

"Believe me," I said. "You'll thank me for this."

7

The next morning I showered and put on clean clothes. I was in the kitchen having cereal and orange juice when Jessica came in wearing a baggy gray sweatshirt and sweatpants. Our parents always slept late on Saturday mornings.

"Did you scrub *everywhere*?" she asked, looking me over.

"Yup."

"Washed your hair?"

"Yup."

"With *shampoo*?"

"Believe it." I held up my hands. "Look, even the nails are clean."

"What nails?" Jessica asked. "You've bitten most of them into nothing."

"Not true," I said. "I just like to keep them short."

"If they were any shorter you wouldn't have any fingernails at all," my sister said, still looking me over. "All clean clothes?"

"You bet."

"Clean underwear?"

"Absolutely."

"Clean *socks*?"

"Yup."

Jessica gave me a skeptical look, as if she didn't believe me. "Want to take a whiff?" I picked up my foot and offered it to her.

"No thanks." She backed away.

"How come you're wearing old sweats?" I asked, pointing at her outfit.

"I don't want you drooling all over my good clothes," she replied.

"I never drool," I said, deeply offended.

"You will after Dr. Paine gets finished with you," my sister said. "Ready to go?"

"Wait a minute," I said. "Aren't you going to have some breakfast first?"

Jessica shook her head. "I never eat before the dentist."

"Maybe *you* don't, but I do," I said. "I don't want to starve until lunch."

"When you get into my body, you can eat anything you — " she caught herself. "No, wait! I take that back! No chocolate, Jake. You hear me? Under no circumstances are you to eat chocolate."

"Why not?" I asked. "Then you and Dandy Dan will have something in common — *Monster Pimples!*"

"Will you stop that?" Jessica snapped. "His complexion isn't *that* bad."

"Are you kidding?" I gasped. "If his zits were any bigger you'd need four-wheel drive to get across his forehead. If his face was flat, they could serve it as a pizza. If one of those zits erupted, it could bury a city."

Jessica smirked. "Very funny. Now, are you ready or not?"

"Almost. I just need to leave Dad a note asking him to drop Sumi off at school for the game. We're playing on the school field." I wrote the note and left it on the refrigerator.

"Okay, I'm ready," I said.

But Jessica had a funny look on her face.

"Now what?" I asked.

"Your mouth," she said.

"What about it?"

"I just realized I'm going to have *your* breath."

"So?"

A shiver seemed to go through my sister. "You have to brush your teeth . . . and gargle with mouthwash."

"*What!?* That's ridiculous."

Jessica crossed her arms and shook her head stubbornly. "Then I'm not switching. I don't care if Dr. Paine pulls every tooth out of my head."

"But *my* body isn't going to the dentist, *yours* is."

My sister stood firm. "Brush and gargle or no deal."

I took a deep breath and let out a long sigh to let her know I thought she was being ridiculous. Then I went back upstairs, brushed my teeth, and gargled. A little while later I came back down. "Happy?"

Jessica stepped toward me. "Exhale."

"What?"

"I said, exhale. I want to check."

"You're really sick, know that?" I said.

"We're trying to be nice to each other, remember?"

"Yeah, right." I exhaled.

My sister stuck her nose closer and sniffed.

"Did I pass?" I asked.

"For now," she answered.

"Well, come on, we better hurry." I started toward the door.

"What's the rush?" Jessica asked as she followed.

"We have to pick up Josh."

Jessica stopped. "Why?"

"Someone has to push the button on the Dirksen Intelligence Transfer System."

"The what?"

"That's what Mr. Dirksen calls his machine," I explained. "Or the DITS for short."

"Well, no way." My sister shook her head. "I'm

27

not doing this if your friend is involved. Forget it."

"What's the problem?" I asked.

"Are you serious, Jake? I don't want people to know you're in my body."

"Well, it's too late," I said. "I already called him. But it's cool. Josh won't tell anybody."

"Yeah, right." Jessica obviously didn't believe me.

"Look," I said. "Has he told anyone that Andy switched bodies with Lance? Or that I switched with the President of the United States?"

"Well, no . . . " my sister admitted.

"Then don't sweat it," I said, holding the front door open. "Josh is the most trustworthy guy I know. He won't tell anyone."

Jessica reluctantly went through the doorway. We stepped into the chilly morning air and started down the sidewalk toward Josh's house.

"You swear he'll be the only one who'll know?" she asked.

"Cross my heart and hope to die."

8

Josh lived a couple of blocks away. Jessica and I went up his front walk and rang the doorbell. The door swung open, but instead of Josh, Andy stood there.

He grinned at me. "Oh, wow! You're gonna switch bodies with your sister? I can't wait to see this!"

Jessica glared at me. "Cross your heart and hope to die? Well, drop dead, Jake."

Andy frowned. "Hey, what's the problem? Aren't you guys gonna do it?"

"Jessica's ticked because Josh wasn't supposed to tell anyone," I explained. "How'd you find out?"

"He told me," Andy said. "I mean, how come you wanted *him* to know and not me?"

"We only needed one person to run the DITS," I explained, looking past Andy and into Josh's house. "Where is Josh anyway?"

"He's coming," Andy said.

A moment later Josh came to the door. When he saw us he clapped his hands together and smiled broadly. "Cool! Are we ready?"

"What are *you* so happy about?" I asked.

"Are you kidding?" Josh closed the door behind him and we headed toward school. "With Jessica in your body there's no way we can lose today, Jake. We're gonna blow the other team right off the field."

"Well, just remember, it's not permanent," I said as we walked. "As soon as the game ends, we're switching back."

"Too bad," Andy muttered.

Josh stopped and sniffed. "Hey, what's that smell?"

I glanced at my sister. "What smell, Josh?"

"I don't know," Josh said. "Kind of smells like a piece of fruit that's been left out in the sun too long."

"Just drop it," Jessica grumbled.

A little while later we got to school. The young writers' conference was scheduled to start in the cafeteria. Everyone was supposed to meet there for an assembly before breaking up into smaller groups. Josh, Andy, Jessica, and I went past the cafeteria doors and started down the empty hall toward Mr. Dirksen's lab.

"Hey, wait a minute!" someone called behind us. "Where do you think you're going?"

9

We froze. Principal Blanco was standing in the hall behind us. He's a short pudgy man with curly black hair, who always wears dark suits.

He crossed his arms and gave us a knowing look. "Jake Sherman and friends, what a surprise."

"A surprise?" I repeated innocently. For some strange reason Principal Blanco thinks my friends and I are troublemakers. I really don't know where he gets that idea.

"What are you kids doing here?" the principal asked.

Everyone's eyes darted at me, as if it was my job to come up with an excuse. "Uh, we're here for the young writers' conference," I said.

Principal Blanco studied me suspiciously. "*You?* When was the last time you even picked up a book, Jake?"

"Well, uh, I figured this might be a good time to start," I said.

Principal Blanco gave me a weary look, then turned to Jessica. "And you're in tenth grade. You don't even go to this school anymore."

"I've decided I want to be a children's book writer," Jessica replied.

Principal Blanco scowled and sniffed the air. "What's that smell?"

"Patchouli oil," I said. "Jessica's wearing it. She thinks it's cool."

"Smells like old skunk," the principal said. "Anyway something tells me you kids are up to something."

I bit my lip nervously. If Principal Blanco threw us out we'd never get to switch bodies. My whole plan would be ruined.

"Honest, Mr. Blanco," I said. "We all want to know more about books and writing and authors."

Andy, Josh, and Jessica nodded in agreement.

Mr. Blanco rubbed his chin pensively. "If you're so interested, name five writers."

"Okay," I said. "Stephen King, R.L. Stine, and uh . . . " I ran out of names and glanced out of the corner of my eye at my friends, hoping they could help.

"Don't help him," Principal Blanco ordered. "I want to see if he can do it himself."

I bit a fingernail. "Uh . . . that Shakespeare guy!"

"Way to go!" Josh cheered.

"That's three," Mr. Blanco said. "You need two more, Jake."

"Uh . . . " Two more writers? That wasn't easy. "Uh . . . I know! Abe Lincoln!"

Mr. Blanco frowned. "He was a president, not a writer."

"But he wrote the Gettysburg Address," I reminded him.

"Doesn't count," said Mr. Blanco.

"How can you say that?" Josh asked. "The Gettysburg Address is a famous piece of writing. It's in all the history books."

"Oh, okay." Our principal sighed. "That's four. But the next one has to be a writer, not a politician."

I shut my eyes and tried to picture the books on my parents' bookshelf. "Uh, Donald Trump!"

Principal Blanco shook his head. "He's not a writer."

"What do you mean?" I asked. "He wrote at least two books."

"Sorry, try again."

I couldn't remember any other authors on my parents' bookshelf, so I tried to remember what was on my bookshelf. They were mostly sports books and I never paid attention to the authors' names. Then I thought of something! "I know, Mad Libs!"

"Who?" Principal Blanco's forehead wrinkled.

"Mad Libs," I said. "He's got tons of books." I turned to the others. "Am I right?"

Josh, Andy, and Jessica nodded enthusiastically.

"I've never heard of him," the principal said.

"Check any bookstore," I said.

"It's true, Mr. Blanco," Andy said.

"And that makes five writers," Josh added.

Our principal nodded reluctantly. "Okay, I'll give you kids the benefit of a great deal of doubt. But you shouldn't be out here in the hall. You should be in the cafeteria with everyone else. Now get going. And I'll be watching you. If I catch you doing anything you're not supposed to be doing, you're out, understand?"

We had no choice, so we filed into the cafeteria where we sat down at a table. All around us little kids and their parents chattered excitedly, waiting for the conference to begin. I picked up a flyer from the table. It said something about the school choir performing in the music room that night.

"Now what?" Josh asked.

"We're running out of time." Jessica tugged nervously on her earlobe. "I'm supposed to be at Dr. Paine's in half an hour."

Suddenly the lights went out and the cafeteria

grew dark. At the other end of the room a writer began to talk and show slides on a screen. I leaned across the table toward the others.

"Time to bail, guys," I whispered. "Under cover of darkness."

10

No one was in the hall. We quickly tiptoed down to Mr. Dirksen's lab. Inside was the Dirksen Intelligence Transfer System. From a large central computer console, dozens of wires led to two reclining chairs. The DITS was supposed to transfer learning from one person to another, but all it really did was switch their bodies.

Jessica hesitated when she saw it. "It looks different."

"Dirksen added the seats," I said. "To make people more comfortable."

My sister tugged at her earlobe. "Maybe this isn't such a good idea."

"You're not going to chicken out *now*?" I gasped. "Not after I got Josh and Andy up early and we snuck past Principal Blanco."

Andy was across the room, looking in the glass tanks where Mr. Dirksen kept various creatures like toads and mice. I noticed that he was giving me a funny look.

"What's with you?" I asked.

"I never thought you'd be so eager to turn into a *girl*," he said.

Neither he nor Josh knew about Sumi. All they knew was that Jessica was going to play football in my body while I went to the dentist in hers.

"What's so bad about being a girl?" Jessica asked.

"Yeah, Andy." Josh smirked. "Jessica's a girl, and she's a better football player than *you*."

"Better than you too, dipwad," Andy shot back.

"Look, guys, we're running out of time," I said. "It's now or never."

My sister stared reluctantly at the DITS. "But what if something goes wrong?"

"I promise you, nothing's going to go wrong," I said.

"Except that she's going to turn into *you*," Andy pointed out. "I mean, talk about your basic fate worse than death."

I glowered at him. "Oh, yeah? Well, you're so thick you stared at a carton of orange juice because it said concentrate."

"You're so dumb you thought a quarterback was a refund," he said.

"Oh, yeah?" I said. "Well, you're so ugly when you were born the doctor slapped your *mother*."

"Your breath is so bad," Andy replied, "the dentist will probably have to give *himself* gas!"

Josh stepped between us. "Okay, guys, can it.

We're running out of time. Don't forget, Andy, with Jessica in Jake's body we're winners. With Jake in Jake's body, we don't stand a chance."

"Thanks, guys," I said with a sniff. "I really appreciate it."

"Well, you have to admit it's true, Jake," Josh said.

I felt my shoulders sag. Maybe it *was* true, but I didn't need my friends to remind me. "Let's just get this over with."

Jessica and I sat in the reclining chairs. Josh stood at the computer and typed on the keyboard.

"Ready?" he asked

"This isn't going to hurt, is it?" my sister asked nervously.

"Well, you might feel a slight sensation, like a pinprick," I said.

"*What?*" Jessica gasped.

"Just a joke," I said. "You know, that's what Dr. Paine always says about the Novocain."

"Yuck, yuck," Jessica groaned. "You're such a comedian, Jake."

"Blast off," Josh said, and pressed a button.

Whump!

Everything went black.

11

"Jake? Jessica?" a distant voice was calling to me, but I couldn't tell from where. I felt like I was in a thick fog.

"Jessica?" the voice sounded clearer.

I opened my eyes and looked up into Andy's face.

"Who are you?" he asked.

"Jake," I said.

Andy gave me a big goofy grin. "Not anymore, *babe*."

I looked down at myself. I was wearing Jessica's gray sweatshirt and sweatpants. The nails on my fingers were long and polished. My hair fell down over my ears.

"Hey, cutie, how about you and me getting together after the game, huh?" Andy winked suggestively.

"How about sticking your face in a bucket of wet concrete?" I replied and got out of the reclining chair. Not far away, Josh was talking to me, I mean, Jessica in my body.

"You feel okay?" he asked me, I mean, her.

"Get real, Josh," Jessica, in my body, replied. "I'm in a body that washes once a month and brushes its teeth even less."

"Hey, no fair," I said. "I did all that stuff this morning, *plus* gargling."

Jessica turned my head and blinked at me in her body. "I don't believe this."

I wasn't used to having all her hair, so I hooked it over my, I mean, her ear. "It's not such a big deal."

"Don't do that to my hair," said my sister, in my body.

"Why not?" I scratched my, I mean, her nose.

"I don't like the way it looks," Jessica said. "And stop scratching."

"Hey, back off," I said. "What're you so uptight about?"

Jessica raised my hands and stared at them. Then she shook my head. "This is too weird. I'm sorry, but I don't like it. All I want to do is get this over with and get back into my body again."

Josh looked at his watch. "You better get going, Jake, er, I mean, Jessica, or you're going to be late for the dentist."

"And we should go out to the field and work on some plays before the game starts," Andy said. He headed for the door.

But my sister and I didn't move. We were still staring at each other.

"Never in a million years would I have believed this," she muttered through my lips.

"Come on, dude." Josh put his hand on my, I mean, her shoulder. "Time to play some ball."

We went out into the hall.

Where Mr. Blanco stood waiting for us.

12

The principal crossed his arms and gave us a knowing look. "Just as I suspected."

"Uh, suspected what?" Andy asked innocently.

"I knew you four were up to something," Mr. Blanco said. "You're supposed to be in the cafeteria. What were you doing in the science lab?"

"Uh . . . " My friends and I shared a wary glance. This time it really looked like we were nailed.

Then Jessica, in my body, spoke up. "We were doing a writing experiment."

"A what?" Mr. Blanco frowned.

"You know, a writing experiment," I said, catching on.

"In the science lab?" Mr. Blanco asked.

"That's where we're supposed to do experiments, right?" Andy asked.

"Well, yes, but . . . in writing?" Mr. Blanco looked really puzzled. As a former gym teacher, he was sort of out of it academically.

"Sure," Josh said. "Today's the young writers' conference, right?"

"Yes, but . . . "

I looked down at Jessica's watch. "I hate to say this, Mr. Blanco, but I'm late for a dentist's appointment."

"And we've got a touch football game," said Andy.

Without waiting for the principal to gather his wits, we hurried past him and out the school doors.

"Phew, that was close." Josh sighed with relief once we got outside. The sun was out, the sky was blue, and the day was gradually warming.

"Yeah, good thinking, Jake," Andy said.

"I beg your pardon?" said Jessica, in my body.

Andy grinned. "Oh, right. I should have known Jake couldn't come up with something like that on his own."

"Some friend." I pressed my sister's lips into a pout.

Jessica turned to me. "You better go or you're going to be late for Dr. Paine."

"And we better get over to the field." Josh pointed to the broad lawn in front of the middle school where we played our touch football games.

"Okay, I'll come to the game as soon as I'm finished," I said, remembering that Sumi would be there.

Andy looked worried. "You're, uh, not gonna want to play, are you?"

"Don't worry, Andy, I'll just come to watch," I assured him, then turned to go.

"Oh, Jessica!" someone shouted. I wheeled around and saw a blond girl wearing a tight pink sweater and a short black skirt. She was hurrying up the sidewalk toward me.

"Oh, no!" Jessica, in my body, gasped in a low voice. "Not Stacy Sloane!"

13

Before I could ask who Stacy Sloane was, she planted herself in front of me and brushed her blond bangs out of her eyes. She was wearing a lot of eye makeup, and her lips were covered with glossy brownish lipstick. Half a dozen earrings dangled from each ear, and her fingers were covered with rings.

"Oh, Jessica," she gushed to me. "I just love what you've done with your hair!"

"Uh, thanks." I swallowed nervously.

"Is it a perm?" Stacy asked.

I glanced out of the corner of my eye at my sister, who nodded my head.

"Oh, yes," I said. "How did you know?"

Stacy scowled. "Well, it's obvious. Yesterday it was straight and brown, and today it's curly and reddish. How else would I know? And I love the highlights. Who did them?"

The only highlights I knew of were the sports highlights on Channel 4 every night.

"Stu Silver," I replied. He was the sports show's host.

"I've never heard of him," Stacy said. "Where is he?"

"Channel Four," I said.

"Is that in town?" Stacy asked.

"It's everywhere," I replied.

"Hmmm." Stacy tapped a shiny brown fingernail against her chin. "Must be a new chain of hair salons. I'm definitely going to try him next time I change hair colors. So what's this I hear about Dan Winters asking you to the carnival?"

"Ahem!" My sister, in my body, suddenly cleared my throat. "Uh, gee, Jessica, you're going to be really late for Dr. Paine."

"You're right!" I gasped, and turned back to Stacy. "I've got to go to the dentist. See you later."

I hurried away down the sidewalk. Next stop, Dr. Paine.

14

Jessica wasn't kidding when she said she had three deep cavities. But once the Novocain kicked in, it wasn't so bad. The only problem was that my, I mean, Jessica's mouth was totally numb and swollen. As soon as Dr. Paine was finished filling the cavities, I tore out of the office and headed back to school. It was just after 10 A.M. and Sumi should have arrived by now.

It had turned into a beautiful fall day. As I hurried toward the field, I could see both teams lined up and facing each other. A familiar voice grunted "Hut one . . . hut two . . . "

I skidded to a stop and watched in disbelief. *I was the quarterback!*

"Hut three . . . hike!" Josh snapped the ball to me, I mean, to Jessica in my body. Everyone on my team took off for the end zone. I watched in awe as I faded back and hurled a bomb!

The football sailed high into the air in a perfect

spiral. Down the field, Andy raced ahead of everyone else.

"I got it! I got it!" he cried.

He caught it in the end zone and scored a TD!

A cheer went up! I'd thrown a touchdown pass! My teammates crowded around me, patting me on the back and congratulating me. I was a hero!

But if I was a hero, how come I was standing on the sidelines in my sister's body?

Because I was only a hero when Jessica was in my body.

What a depressing thought. I felt my, I mean, Jessica's shoulders sag.

But then I brightened. No one knew!

Then I felt bummed again. No one except Jessica, Josh, Andy, and me.

Meanwhile, the teams were lining up for the kickoff, and I remembered why I'd hurried back to the field. Standing a dozen yards away was a tall girl with long shining black hair. She was wearing jeans and a white shirt. A slight breeze blew her hair into her face. The guys on the field were giving her puzzled looks and whispering to each other. You could tell from their expressions that they didn't know who she was or why she was watching their game.

But I knew.

I walked over and stopped near her. I could feel my sister's heart pounding rapidly in her chest and goose bumps on her arms.

"Huhho." I tried to say hello but my sister's mouth was still numb.

Sumi turned and pulled her hair away from her face. I felt my sister's jaw drop. Not only did she have long, shimmering black hair, but pale, soft skin and dark, gorgeous eyes. *She was beautiful!*

"Did you say something?" she asked.

"Uh-huh." I nodded and held out my sister's hand. "Hom Hake."

Sumi gave me a funny look. "Maybe you should try speaking English."

"Ha *ham* sheecking Engluch," I said. "Buh ha hush cahme hrum huh hentish."

Sumi frowned. "You just came from what?"

"Hentish." I opened my sister's mouth, stuck a finger in like a drill, and made a drilling sound. "*Huuuuunnnnnnnuuuuunnnnnnuuuunnnn!*"

"A dentist?" Sumi guessed.

I nodded eagerly and pointed at my sister's mouth. "Muh mouf ith hall thowhen."

"Swollen?" Sumi guessed.

I nodded some more. "Hooh sheeck goo Engluch."

Sumi smiled, revealing beautiful straight white teeth. "Thank you. I study hard in school. Some of it is still a little strange to me. My name is Sumiko, but everyone calls me Sumi."

"Hom Hake."

"Hake?"

49

I shook my sister's head. "Juuhhh . . . Jjjjjjj . . . ake."

Sumi looked surprised. "Did you say, Jake?"

"Yesh!" I nodded happily.

Then she frowned. "I thought Jake was a boy."

Ooops!

15

In my excitement, I'd forgotten whose body I was in. "Ha menth ha ham Hake's hister."

"Jake's sister?"

I nodded. "Hehika."

"Hehika?" Sumi repeated.

"*Hehika.*"

"Hehika?"

I shook my sister's head in frustration. As long as my, I mean, Jessica's mouth was swollen and numb, Sumi couldn't understand me.

Loud shouts came from the game. Sumi and I turned to see me, I mean, Jessica in my body, intercept a pass thrown by the other team's quarterback. Once again, my teammates crowded around and patted me on the shoulder.

"Hat's Hake!" I clapped my sister's hands.

"The one who just caught the ball?" Sumi asked.

"Yesh!"

51

"He's very good," Sumi said. "I noticed him right away."

That made me feel good. "He's huh hery hreat atheet," I said. "Huh hest in huh hool."

"The best in the school?" Sumi repeated.

I nodded.

"You must be very proud of him," Sumi said.

"Yesh! And he's huh hery hood hother."

"A very good brother?" Sumi was starting to understand me better. "You're lucky. Sometimes younger brothers can be a big pain."

"Not Hake," I said. "He's huh hest."

"I am looking forward to meeting him," Sumi said.

All right! I had to smile to myself. The plan was working! Sumi thought I was a great athlete. She was looking forward to meeting me. After the game Jessica and I would switch back into our own bodies and everything would be perfect.

"Yo, Jessica!" Just then someone called out my sister's name.

A guy with dark hair was strolling toward us.

His blue shirt was neatly pressed and his pants had creases.

He didn't have the greatest complexion.

Oh, no! It was Dandy Dan Winters!

16

I was gripped with terror. What if Dan put his arm around my waist and tried to kiss me?

Barf City!

I clenched my sister's teeth and crossed her arms tightly, praying he wouldn't touch me.

"Hi, Jessica." As Dan joined us, his eyes focused on Sumi.

"Hi, Han." I braced myself, still waiting for his arm to go around my sister's waist.

But it didn't.

Instead, he stared at Sumi like he was in some kind of daze. Finally he turned to me and said, "So, how's it going?"

"Hohay," I answered.

"What are you doing here?" he asked.

"Hotching Hake hay," I replied.

Dan scowled. *"What?"*

I pointed at my, I mean, Jessica's, mouth. "Hi hust hame hum huh hentist."

"Huh?" He still didn't understand.

"Huuuuunnnnnnuuuuunnnnnuuuunnnn!" I pointed my sister's finger at her mouth and made the drilling sound.

Dan stared at me like I'd lost my mind, then shot another glance at Sumi. "So, uh, who's your friend?"

Something in the tone of his voice, plus the way he kept looking at Sumi, gave me a funny feeling. Was he interested in her? Was that why he hadn't put his arm around my sister's waist or tried to kiss me?

All at once I didn't want to introduce him to Sumi.

"Hahguh wahguh buguh." I pointed at my, I mean, Jessica's mouth again and mumbled some nonsense he couldn't understand.

"What did you say?" Dan frowned.

"Wiguh wahguh wooguh."

"Gee, Jessica, what's wrong with you?"

Sumi turned to us and brushed her long beautiful hair away from her face. "She just came from the dentist."

"Oh!" Dan smiled and offered her his hand. "Hi, I'm Dan Winters."

Sumi shook his hand. "I am Sumiko, but everyone calls me Sumi."

"Sumi? That's a really pretty name," Dan said. "Where are you from?"

"Tokyo."

"Wow, what brings you here?" he asked.

"I have come with my father, who is doing business with Mr. Sherman. I am visiting Jake and his family for the day."

"*Jake Sherman?*" Dan made a face. "That little dwee — "

I poked him in the ribs with my, I mean, Jessica's, elbow.

"Ooof!" Dan doubled over. Then he straightened up and scowled at me. I made a face. He got the message.

"So, uh, how do you know Jake?" he asked.

"We are pen pals," Sumi replied. "We have been exchanging E-mail."

"Then you've never actually met him?" Dan asked.

"This is the first time," Sumi replied.

"I see." Dan smiled to himself. I could tell that he was cooking up a scheme in that slime bucket brain of his.

Out on the field another shout went up. We watched as Jessica, in my body, made an amazing, diving catch in the end zone for another touchdown.

"Yay, Hake!" I shouted and pumped my sister's fist.

"Very good!" Sumi clapped her hands excitedly.

"Amazing!" Dan gasped. "Jake usually rots at football."

"Rots?" Sumi turned to him. "I am not familiar

with that term when it is applied to people."

"It's just a saying," Dan explained. "It means — "

"He's heally hrate!" I cut in.

"Really great?" Sumi nodded. "Yes, then Jake certainly rots."

"But that's not what it — " Dan began.

Before he could finish, I grabbed him by the arm and yanked him away.

Dan gave me a surprised look as I dragged him out of earshot. "What's with you, Jessica?"

"*Heep hor ophions who horhelf!*" I hissed from between Jessica's clenched teeth.

"Huh?" He looked like he didn't know what in the world I was saying.

Luckily the numbness from the Novocain was starting to fade. I really concentrated and was able to whisper "*Keep your opinions to yourselsh.*"

Dan frowned. "Why?"

"I don't like hit when you shay bad hings about my sisther," I said.

"*Sister?*" Dan looked totally confused.

" . . . er, I meant, my buther," I said.

"But you're always putting him down," Dan said.

"Not anymore," I whispered through my sister's lips.

"Okay, okay." Dan seemed impatient to end our conversation and get back to Sumi again. "Hey, Jessica," he said in a loud voice. "I have an idea.

Why don't we ask Sumi if she wants to come to the carnival with us this afternoon?"

Sumi go with my sister and Dan? That was the *last thing in the world* I wanted. But before I could say so, Sumi turned to us, her eyes widening with delight.

"Did you say 'carnival'?" she gasped.

17

"That's right," Dan said. "Carnival."

Sumi clasped her hands together excitedly. "I would *love* to go to a carnival!"

"Great!" Dan turned to me. "What do you say, Jessica? It's okay if Sumi comes with us, isn't it? I mean, she *really* wants to go."

Darn it! Dan had me on the spot. If I said no I'd be disappointing Sumi. If I said yes, he'd get to spend all afternoon with her.

Fortunately, my sister's mouth was almost back to normal by now. "Well, the only problem is that Sumi really came here to visit Jake. So I think we should wait and ask him."

From the sly glimmer in Dan's eye I could tell he was still scheming. "That's the part I don't get. Isn't Jake a little *young* for Sumi?"

"Oh, no," Sumi said. "Jake is seventeen. He told me so himself."

"*Seventeen!?*" Dan cried. "That runt? No

way! He can't be more than fourteen."

Sumi frowned and looked at me. "Is this true, Jessica?"

Things were going from bad to worse. The truth was, I'd done more than just lie to Sumi about my athletic abilities. I'd also lied about my age.

"Well . . . " *What could I say?*

"Look at him." Dan pointed at me out in the field. "Does that little twerp look like he's seventeen?"

Sumi stared for a moment, then turned to me in my sister's body again. "Jessica, how old is your brother?"

There was no point in lying. She could see I wasn't as old as I'd said I was.

"Well, actually, he is fourteen," I admitted. But then I added, "He's very mature for his age."

"Yeah, right." Dan smirked. "How old are *you,* Sumi?"

"I'm sixteen," she said, frowning. "I don't understand why Jake would say he was seventeen if he is only fourteen."

"Well, that's pretty simple," Dan said with a chuckle. "He lives here and you live in Tokyo. He probably never dreamed that you'd actually — "

I had no intention of letting him finish *that* sentence. For once I was glad my sister had long arms and pointy elbows.

"*Ooof!*" The next thing Dan knew, he was doubled over again, holding his stomach and gasping in pain.

"What happened?" Sumi asked, alarmed.

"Gee, I don't know." I shrugged my sister's shoulders innocently. "Maybe it was something he ate."

18

Out on the field the game ended. My team-mates were patting me on the back and congratulating me on my great game.

"You were incredible, Jake!"

"Wow, guy, you're the best!"

"Thanks, guys." Jessica, in my body, basked in the attention. Even the captain of the other team came over and shook her, I mean, my hand.

"You were amazing, Jake," he said.

"That's really nice of you to say," my sister replied.

"Next time we play, I'm gonna make sure you're on my team," the other captain said.

I watched myself glow with pride. If only that was really me. I wondered what they'd say if they knew they were congratulating Jessica in my body. Then Josh, Andy, and Jessica came over to Sumi, Dan, and me.

Josh and Andy gave Sumi curious looks. After all, I'd never told them about her.

"Boys, this is Sumi." I introduced her to them.

Sumi said hello and then turned to Jessica in my body. She wasn't smiling. "So we finally get to meet, Jake."

"Did you get to see much of the game?" asked Jessica in my body.

"Oh, yes," said Sumi. "You really rot."

Jessica, in my body, blinked and looked shocked.

"So, Jake," said Dan, who didn't know that my sister and I had switched bodies. "How does it feel to finally meet your pen pal from the other side of the world?"

"*Pen pal?*" Andy scowled.

"Uh, great," replied Jessica in my body.

"You don't feel a little awkward?" Dan asked.

Jessica furrowed my brow. "No, why should I?"

"Maybe because you told Sumi you were seventeen when you're really only fourteen," Dan said.

I watched as an astonished expression appeared on my face. Jessica, in my body, glared at me in hers, as if waiting for me to come up with an explanation.

"Well, I mean, it was just a little fib," I said.

"It's very honorable of you to try to make excuses for your brother, Jessica," Sumi said to me. "I admit that I'm a little disappointed. But still, I'm glad to be here." Then she turned back to my sister in my body. "Jake, your sister Jessica and her friend Dan have asked me to join them at the carnival this afternoon. Would that be okay?"

Jessica widened my eyes. She looked at Dan, then turned to me and glared again. They may have been my eyes, but there was murder in them.

19

"Uh, could you excuse us for a second?" Jessica, in my body, asked everyone. The next thing I knew, my sister took me aside.

"What is going on?" she hissed in a low voice the others couldn't hear.

"I couldn't help it," I whispered back and tucked her hair behind her ear. "Zitface, er, I mean, Dan mentioned the carnival and Sumi got all excited. She really wants to go. What was I supposed to do?"

"First of all, stop tucking my hair behind my ear!" Jessica whispered heatedly. "Second, I don't want her coming to the carnival with Dan and me."

I untucked her hair and whispered. "Neither do I. But I can't say no. It wouldn't be polite."

"Oh, really?" hissed Jessica in my body. "Look at Dan!"

I glanced back at Dan. He was gazing at Sumi with a rapt expression and dreamy eyes.

"He's not supposed to look at *her* that way," Jessica sputtered. "He's supposed to look at *me* that way."

"You mean, me," I whispered, reminding her that at the moment I was her and she was me.

Jessica rolled my eyes. "Whoever."

"By the way," I said. "How did it feel to be a sports hero?"

Jessica smiled. "Great! Did you see how the captain of the other team asked me to play for him next time?"

I nodded, suddenly feeling a little jealous.

"It sure is different from being a girl," my sister went on. "Half the time, when I do well in sports, the other girls just snigger and make fun of me. And even if they appreciate what I've done, they don't congratulate me nearly as much."

"See how important sports is to a guy?" I asked.

Jessica, in my body, nodded. "I feel really sorry for you."

Before I could tell her that I didn't want her pity, Josh and Andy joined us.

"How come you guys went off alone to talk?" Josh whispered. "What's the problem?"

"Uh, it's private," replied my sister, in my body. "What do you want?"

"We want to know if there's any chance you'd stay in Jake's body until the next game," Andy said in a hushed voice. "We really ruled out there today."

Jessica didn't answer. I could see that she was seriously considering it.

"You guys aren't really serious, are you?" I asked my friends.

Andy bit his lip. "Well, yeah. Did you see how you played today? You were awesome."

"But what about the real me?" I asked. "What about when we're *not* playing football? Doesn't our friendship mean anything? Is sports all you guys really care about?"

"You're right," Josh admitted. "It's not *just* sports. It's *winning* at sports that really counts."

"But what about our *friendship*?" I asked.

"We could still be friends," Josh said.

"But we'd be winners too," Andy added.

"In fact, that would probably make us even better friends," Josh pointed out.

"I can't believe this!" I groaned. "You guys don't care about me. All you care about is sports."

Jessica in my body laughed. "Look who's talking!"

"You stay out of this," I growled.

But Jessica shook my head. "You're so typical. Last night you insisted that sports is everything in life. Now you can't believe that your friends feel that way, too."

I glared at my sister in my body, but she smiled back, knowing she was right.

"Ahem!" Andy cleared his throat. "So, uh, back to my original question. Is there any chance you guys would stay in these bodies until the end of football season?"

My sister, in my body, gave me a searching look. It was obvious she was still considering it.

"You can't be serious," I said.

"I really had a lot of fun out there," she said.

"Well, I'm *not* having a lot of fun, okay?" I sputtered. "Being you is a big fat drag."

"Give it a chance," Jessica said.

I shook her head vehemently. "Forget it."

Andy turned to Josh and shrugged. "Well, I tried."

Josh sighed and pointed at his wristwatch. "In that case we better get back into school."

He was right. If Jessica and I were going to switch back to our own bodies, we had to do it before the young writers' conference ended and school closed.

"What are we gonna tell Sumi?" I whispered.

Jessica, in my body, turned to Dan and Sumi, who appeared to be deep in their own conversation. "Sumi?"

"Yes, Jake?" Sumi looked up.

"Uh, Jessica and I have to run into school for a moment," my sister said. "Would you mind waiting?"

A big smile appeared on Dan's face. "Hey, no

problem, Jake. Take your time. I'll stay with Sumi."

Jessica blinked my eyes. Then she turned back to me. "Jake," she whispered, tugging on my earlobe. "You have to do something for me."

"What?" I whispered back.

"Go over to Dan and kiss him on the cheek," she said.

20

I looked at my sister, in my body, like she was crazy. *"Are you out of your mind!"* I hissed.

"Please, Jake?" she bit my lip and begged.

"Why?" I asked.

"To remind him who his real date for this afternoon is," she whispered.

"If you want to remind him who his date is, *you* kiss him," I whispered back.

"I can't," she whispered. "He thinks I'm Jake."

"Well, he may think that, but I'm really Jake, and there's no way I'm kissing him," I said.

"But he doesn't know you're Jake," she said. "He thinks you're Jessica."

"Well, *I* know I'm Jake," I sputtered. "And Josh and Andy know it too."

"Jake, please!"

"No."

"Jaaaaake, pleeeease!" my sister in my body whined. "Just a little peck on the cheek?"

"Never! Not in a million years! I don't care

whose body I'm in. I wouldn't put my lips on his scuzzy pimply cheeks for a billion gazillion dollars. Especially in front of my friends." I admit I got a little excited.

Jessica, in my body, glanced back at Dandy Dan again. I could see that she was really upset. To tell you the truth, I felt bad for her. Or maybe it was just that I was a little upset, too. I mean, Sumi was supposed to be *my* friend. I didn't like Dan drooling all over her any more than my sister did. But now that Sumi knew I'd lied about my age, I felt really humiliated. In a strange kind of way I almost wished she *would* go off with Dan. Because every second I spent with her was a second of her looking at me and knowing that I hadn't told the truth.

21

The young writers' conference must have been coming to an end because everyone was in the cafeteria listening to some writer with a beard talk about how he'd needed help with reading when he was a kid. Josh, Andy, Jessica, and I snuck past the cafeteria doors, then down the hall and back to the science lab.

"Okay," Josh said, closing the lab door softly behind him. "Let's make this quick. I don't want to get nailed by Principal Blanco."

Jessica and I quickly got into the reclining chairs. Josh went over to the computer console and began typing. Andy was on the other side of the room looking at the animals again. Then he glanced over at me. "Just out of curiosity, Jake, how did *you* like being a girl?"

"It's not such a big deal," I said, shrugging my sister's shoulders.

Josh looked up from the computer. "What about wearing perfume?"

Oddly, I'd forgotten about that. "You get used to it," I replied. "After a while you hardly even notice."

My sister, in my body, gave me a funny look. "That's scary, Jake."

"Maybe he'll still wear perfume after he changes back," Andy quipped.

"Very funny," I grumbled.

Josh finished typing and put his finger on the button. "Everyone ready?"

"Yeah," I said.

"How about you, Jessica?" Josh asked.

She didn't answer. She had twisted my body around in her chair and was staring out the window.

"Jessica?" Josh tried to get her attention. "I asked if you were ready."

"Wait a minute." Jessica, in my body, got out of the chair and went to the window.

Josh frowned. "Now what?"

"Something must be going on." I slid out of my chair and joined my sister at the window. Outside Dan and Sumi were strolling across the school yard, talking. Dan was standing close to Sumi, and he kept glancing at her with that mushy look.

"Uh-oh." Andy joined us at the window. "Dan the Man's on the make."

Jessica put my hands on my hips and narrowed my eyes. "I don't like this."

Just then Dan pointed at something across the school yard. Sumi shook her head as if she couldn't see what he was pointing at. So Dan slipped his arm around Sumi's shoulders to help turn her in the direction he was pointing.

"What a fake!" Andy gasped. "He just wants an excuse to put his arm around her shoulder!"

Jessica started tugging at my earlobe. "Now I *really* don't like this!"

"Stop tugging at my earlobe like that," I said. "You're gonna stretch it out."

I don't think my sister even heard me. "I can't believe him," she said to myself. "I just *can't* believe him!"

"I *told* you he was slime," I said.

Outside, kids and their parents began to cross the school yard.

"The conference must be over," Josh warned us. "We better switch you guys back into your own bodies before they close the school."

I headed back to the DITS. Jessica, in my body, was still standing by the window, making my eyes bulge out of my head, and clenching and unclenching my fists.

"I can't believe him," she kept muttering. "I really can't believe him!"

"Come on, Jessica," Josh said. "We're running out of time."

My sister, in my body, returned to her seat.

Once again Josh typed something on the computer. "Ready?"

Jessica and I nodded.

"Okay," Josh said. "Three . . . two . . . "

Just then the door opened and Principal Blanco stepped into the lab.

22

"Let me guess." Our principal arched a skeptical eyebrow. "You're doing another writing experiment?"

"Uh . . . " Jessica, Andy, Josh, and I exchanged panicked looks. Josh reached toward the red button on the DITS.

"Get away from that machine, Josh," the principal ordered. "You know you're not supposed to fool around with it."

Josh stepped away from the DITS.

"And you two." Mr. Blanco turned to my sister and me. "Out of those chairs, now!"

We got out of the chairs. Mr. Blanco crossed his arms. "All right, kids. I'm waiting for an explanation. And it better be good."

"Well, you see . . . " Andy began, but then trailed off.

"It all started when . . . " Jessica, in my body, couldn't continue either.

Mr. Blanco turned to Josh. "Want to give it a try?"

Josh shook his head. He wasn't even going to bother making up an excuse. Mr. Blanco looked at me next. "How about you, Jessica?"

I bent my sister's head and stared down at the floor. "It's all my fault, Mr. Blanco."

The principal looked surprised. "Go on, Jessica."

"Well, if you *really* want to know the truth," I continued, "I just really miss middle school. It's not the same over at the high school. It's so big and impersonal over there. I wanted to come back here because I have such fond memories."

Mr. Blanco blinked with surprise. "I see."

"I mean, it's not like we were doing anything wrong," I said as sincerely as possible. "I just wanted to come back and feel like an eighth-grader again."

Mr. Blanco pressed his lips together thoughtfully. "I guess it's not easy growing up."

I nodded Jessica's head sadly. Out of the corner of my sister's eye I caught my friends giving each other amazed looks, as if they couldn't believe I was going to talk my way out of this.

Meanwhile, Mr. Blanco rubbed his chin thoughtfully and seemed moved by my words. "You really loved it here, didn't you, Jessica?"

"Yes." I nodded my sister's head some more.

"You'd probably like to come back again," Mr. Blanco said. "Am I right?"

"Oh, yes, Mr. Blanco," I said dramatically. "More than anything!"

"Well, good," the principal said. "Because Monday morning I'm going to call Principal Smiley over at the high school and arrange for you to come back."

Huh? That didn't make sense.

"Uh, er, that's great," I replied uncertainly.

In my body, Jessica muttered unhappily. "No, it's not, meatbrain."

"It's not?" I frowned.

Mr. Blanco nodded. "I think what your brother means, Jessica, is that by the time your week of detention is over, you probably will have had enough of this place for a long, long time."

A week of detention? I felt my sister's jaw drop.

But wait! By then Jessica and I would have switched back into our own bodies. I wouldn't be serving that detention, *Jessica would!* I put my sister's hand over her mouth to hide her smile.

"You see, Jessica," the principal continued. "When I told you before that I didn't want you wandering around school, I meant it. Just because you're a tenth-grader at the high school doesn't mean that you're not subject to school rules."

"Uh, excuse me, Mr. Blanco?" Jessica, in my body, said.

The principal turned. "Yes, Jake?"

"It's really not Jessica's fault," my sister, in my body, said. "It's really my fault. I'm the one who insisted that she come back in here again. If anyone gets a week's detention, it should be me, Jake Sherman."

Principal Blanco blinked. "Did I hear you correctly, Jake? *You're* volunteering to serve detention for your sister?"

"It's only fair," my sister in my body said.

"No, it's not!" I gasped in my sister's body. "You were right in the first place, Mr. Blanco. I, Jessica Sherman, should serve detention. I broke the rules and I should face my punishment like a man."

Principal Blanco frowned.

"Ahem!" Josh cleared his throat.

"Uh, I meant, like a *woman*," I quickly corrected myself.

My sister, in my body, turned to me. "I insist I serve it, Jessica."

"No, no, Jake," I replied. "As your big sister I should have had better judgment. I must be taught a lesson!"

"But you only did it for me," Jessica insisted.

Jessica, in my body, and I, in hers, argued back and forth.

"Stop!" Principal Blanco finally yelled. "I don't

know what's gotten into you two, but forget it. And forget about detention. Now I don't know who to give it to. But this is the last time I'm going to tell you to leave. I have to close the school. If I see you back here again, the next step will be a *month's* detention!"

Mr. Blanco really wanted us to leave. But we couldn't. We had to switch first. I had to get my body back. And that meant switching *now*!

"Oh, please, Mr. Blanco," I begged. "Can't I just stay *a little* longer?"

The principal gave me an amazed look. "Jessica, didn't you hear what I just said?"

"But — " I gasped.

"No buts, Jessica." Mr. Blanco firmly waved us toward the door. "You either leave right now or I'll make sure you get that month's detention."

"But you don't understand," I gasped.

"Yes, he *does*." I felt a sharp stab of pain in the ribs as Jessica, in my body, came close and gave me a poke.

Principal Blanco smiled. "Well, I see that at least Jake has some sense."

23

"Thanks, Jake, thanks a lot!" my sister muttered angrily in my body as we walked down the hall toward the school doors. "You were ready to let me get a month's detention."

"Hey!" I shot back. "It wasn't *my* fault! We would have switched by now if you weren't so worried about what Dandy Dan was doing with Sumi."

"Oh, sure." Jessica rolled my eyes. "Blame it on everyone else except yourself. You're *such* a typical male."

I stopped and glared at her in my body. Then I put one hand on her hip and bent the other in a feminine way. "And *you're* such a typical girl. All you can think about is some dumb guy who doesn't even *care* about you."

"Yes, he does!" Jessica, in my body, insisted as we went through the school doors and outside.

"Oh, yeah?" I said. "Then how come he was putting the moves on Sumi?"

"He wasn't putting the moves on her," Jessica, in my body, insisted. "He was just being friendly."

Now that we were outside, I looked around the school yard for Dan and Sumi.

But they were gone.

"Oh, yeah," I said with a smirk. "He sure was being friendly. So friendly he took her and left without us."

Jessica, in my body, spun around, looking for them. "I don't believe it!"

Meanwhile, Josh looked at his watch. "I'm going home. It's time for lunch and I'm starved. You guys want to come?"

"I'll come," Andy said.

But my sister, in my body, had started marching down the sidewalk in the opposite direction.

"Hey!" I shouted. "Where are you going?"

"To town," Jessica replied without stopping.

"Why?" I asked.

"Why do you think, Jake?"

"Uh . . . you think that's where Dan and Sumi went?"

"Amazing deduction, Jake," my sister called back. "It's reassuring to know that my brain still works, even with *you* in my body."

I turned back to Josh and Andy. "I better go with her. I'll catch you guys later."

"What about getting back into your body?" Andy asked.

81

My sister rolled my eyes toward the sky. "Guess we'll have to wait until Monday morning."

"No, wait!" I said. "I read something when we were in school before. The choir's singing here tonight. We can come back then."

"But that means we have to spend the whole day in each other's bodies," Jessica said.

"It's better than spending the whole *weekend*," I replied.

Andy grinned. "Have fun today, *babe*."

"Very funny, Andy," I said, then ran down the sidewalk until I caught up with my sister in my body.

"I can't believe I'm going to be stuck in your body the *whole* day," she grumbled as she walked quickly toward town in my body.

"Hey, give it a rest already," I said. "Being stuck in *your* body is no picnic either."

A few moments later we got into town. Jessica stopped at the intersection of Main and North, the two busiest streets. She put my hands on my hips and looked around. "We better split up," she said. "I'll go down Main Street. You go up North Street."

"What should I do if I find them?" I asked.

"Stop it," Jessica, in my body, said.

"Stop what?"

"Stop biting my fingernails."

Startled, I pulled my sister's fingers away from

her mouth. I hadn't been aware that I was biting them.

"I'm depending on you not to mess up my nails," Jessica said sternly. "Now we better look for Dan and Sumi. I don't want them getting too friendly."

Jessica turned and headed down Main Street looking in the windows of the shops.

"How am I supposed to keep them from getting too friendly?" I called after her.

"Use your imagination," she yelled back.

"But . . ."

Too late. My sister, in my body, strode away. I turned and started up North Street, checking out the shops, and wondering exactly how I was supposed to keep Dandy Dan from getting too friendly with Sumi. Since I was in Jessica's body, I figured I would be expected to do some girl kind of thing, like cry or claw Dan's eyeballs out of his head. But since I was really a guy inside a girl's body, I felt more inclined to do a guy kind of thing — like cry, claw his eyes out *and* break his nose.

"Oh, Jessica!" Without warning, someone grabbed my, I mean, Jessica's arm and yanked me into a store. It was Stacy Sloane! I looked around and felt a cold shiver run down my sister's spine. Stacy had just pulled me into a boutique called Scarcely Hers.

24

Scarcely Hers is this store that sells ladies clothes and swimsuits. In the window are mannequins wearing tight sweaters and skimpy skirts, or tiny bikinis. These things can't possibly do what clothes are supposed to do, namely:

1) Keep you warm.
2) Keep you covered up.

Normally, my friends and I walk past Scarcely Hers as fast as we can and avoid looking in the window (well, sometimes, if no one is around, we might peek in as we go past). But we never, ever stop. To stop and look in the window, even at night when no one else is around, means that you might be exposed to deadly Girl Rays. Scarcely Hers is a glowing nuclear reactor of girl stuff. It's practically fatal to boys.

And forget about going in. There is no way any self-respecting fourteen-year-old guy would even *set foot* in a place like that. You'd be instantly contaminated!

Your growth would probably be stunted.

You'd definitely be scarred for life.

Now I was standing in Scarcely Hers with Stacy. We were surrounded by racks of women's swimsuits and clothes. The air was sweetly perfumed. New Age whale music was floating out of a couple of speakers on the walls. It was bad enough being in my sister's body. But being in her body *and* being in that store was total Girl Ray overload!

I felt like I couldn't breathe.

I was drowning in girl stuff!

"I'm so glad I found you," Stacy said.

"I have to go," I gasped. I lurched toward the door, but Stacy had my sister's arm in a vice grip.

"You can't go!" she cried, pulling me back.

"Why not?" I asked.

"I need a fashion consultant."

"Then find one," I said, trying to pull free.

"But *you're* my fashion consultant," she said. "You always help me with a second opinion."

"If you need a second opinion, go to a doctor!"

Stacy held onto my sister's arm and grinned at me. "That's a good one, Jessica. By the way, I looked everywhere for Channel Four and couldn't find it."

"Huh?" I had no idea what she was talking about.

"You know, that place where you got your

highlights done," she said. "By that Stu guy."

"Oh, yeah." Now I remembered what she was talking about. "Uh, it's out at the mall."

"Oh." Stacy nodded, then frowned. "Wait a minute. Aren't you supposed to be going to the carnival with Dan?"

"That's why I have to leave right now. If I don't I'll be late." What I really had to do was get out of that store. Mr. Dirksen's machine had already turned me into a girl on the *outside*. Spending another minute in Scarcely Hers would probably turn me into a girl on the *inside*. I strained toward the door, but Stacy wouldn't let go of my sister's arm.

"But you can't go like *that*," she said.

I looked down and realized I was wearing the old baggy gray sweats Jessica had put on that morning.

"What time's your date?" Stacy asked.

"Uh . . . right now. That's why I have to go." I tried to leave again, but Stacy still had a firm grip on my, I mean, my sister's arm.

"I don't know what's gotten into you, Jessica," she said. "You can't go on a date with Dan looking like that. I won't let you. It's my duty as your friend to help you. Forget about *my* fashion problems, we have to do something about *you*."

Still holding my sister's arm tightly, Stacy started thumbing through the racks of short skirts and teeny blouses. Meanwhile, I could feel the Girl Rays permeating the outer layers of my sister's body, trying to get at me.

This was bad. Another five minutes in this place and I'd probably forget that I ever was a boy.

"That's really nice of you, Stacy," I gasped. "But I'm really short of money. I don't know when I'll be able to pay you back."

"I know you, Jessica," Stacy said. "You always pay back your debts. Besides, I still owe you for that sweater of yours I ruined."

"Wha . . . ?" I didn't know what she was talking about.

"The one my mom threw in the dryer and shrunk."

"That old rag?" I tried to play it down. "It was hardly worth a thing."

"Oh, stop it, Jessica," Stacy said. "It was brand-new. Not only that, but now I can finally pay you back for all the times you helped me pick out clothes. How about this?"

She pulled out a skimpy skirt and a sort of semi see-through blouse. It practically glowed with red-hot Girl Rays!

"Oh, gosh!" I gasped. "I can't wear *that*!"

"Why not?" Stacy asked.

"You can almost see through it."

Stacy smiled. "No prob, Jess. We'll just make sure you wear a cute little bikini top underneath."

25

The next thing I knew, Stacy was nudging me toward the dressing rooms in the back of the store. *A cute little bikini top?* This was bad, *really* bad. Continued exposure to such high levels of Girl Rays had to be harmful to my health. Besides, Jessica and I had a deal. I wasn't allowed to look, and neither was she.

"Stacy, I can't. Really, I have to go."

"I know," Stacy said, holding up the skimpy skirt and see-through blouse. "That's why you have to try these on fast."

"Why can't I just wear what I'm wearing?" I asked.

"You're not serious." Stacy put the skirt and blouse in my sister's hands and pushed me into a changing room. She closed the door behind me. "Do you really think Dan wants to see you in baggy sweats?"

"Why should it matter?" I asked.

"Jessica, are you feeling all right?" Stacy asked

on the other side of the dressing room door. "You don't sound like yourself."

"I'm a new me," I said and pushed on the door. But it wouldn't open.

"You may be a new you," Stacy said, "but believe me. Dan's still the same old Dan. He wants the girl he dates to look gorgeous. Stay here. I'm going to find you a bikini."

I looked around the dressing room. It was small and brightly lit. The side walls had big mirrors on them. The back wall had a wooden bench built into it. I looked down at the skirt and blouse Stacy had given me. *No way*, I thought. *Forget it. I'm out of here.*

I pushed open the dressing room door. But Stacy was standing there with a bikini made out of some kind of shiny silver material.

"Isn't this just perfect?" she asked, dumping the bikini in my sister's hands and pushing the dressing room door closed again. "Now hurry!"

This was turning into a nightmare. Not only was I stuck in my sister's body in a dressing room in the glowing center of the Girl Ray Universe, but now I was supposed to dress up in short tight clothes and a silver bikini!

"I just don't see why looks have to be so important," I said through the door.

"You're right, Jessica, they shouldn't be," Stacy agreed outside. "But they are and there's nothing we can do about it."

This was getting absurd. The *last* thing I wanted to do was look good for Dandy Dan. Frankly, given the choice between dating Dan or my dog, Lance, there was no choice. Lance won.

I put the clothes on the bench and pushed against the door.

It didn't budge.

"Forget it, Jessica," Stacy called from the other side. "I'm not letting you out until you put on those clothes."

"Are you serious?" I gasped.

"I'm doing this for your own good," Stacy said. "Someday you'll thank me."

26

The dressing room walls were only about six and a half feet high. Above that was four feet of open space before the ceiling. Suddenly I had an idea. There was one good thing about being stuck in my sister's body.

I was taller.

I stepped on the bench, reached up and grabbed the top of a side wall. Then I did a pull-up and got my sister's chin over the top. Now I could see down into the dressing room next to mine.

It was empty!

"I hope you're changing, Jessica," Stacy called from outside my dressing room. "You don't have much time, you know."

"I know," I called back. "Don't worry, I won't be long."

I slowly inched one leg over the top of the wall

and into the next dressing room. A moment later
I was straddling the wall between the two dressing rooms. All I had to do was slip down into the
second dressing room and . . .

The door to the second dressing room opened!

27

A big fat woman stepped into the dressing room, carrying an armful of dresses.

I held my breath.

She didn't see me straddling the wall above.

Now I had a choice. I could go back into my old dressing room, where Stacy wouldn't let me out until I'd changed into those absurd girl clothes. Or, I could deal with the BFW.

I quickly made my decision, and whispered, "Uh, excuse me."

The BFW turned and stared up at me. Her eyes bugged out and her mouth started to open.

I quickly pressed a finger to my sister's lips. "Shh!" Then I lowered myself into her dressing room.

The BFW watched me warily. "Who are you?" she whispered nervously. "What are you doing in here?"

In her arms was that pile of dresses. I got an idea. "I'm the fashion consultant."

She scowled. "Really?"

"Yes. My job is to help you select the right clothes. For instance." I pointed at a bright purple dress in the pile in her arms. "This one is all wrong for you."

The BFW's forehead wrinkled. "You think?"

"Yes, it doesn't go with your natural coloring at all," I said.

"Really!?" The BFW's eyes widened.

"Yes, you strike me as being a very earthy person," I said. "You should stick with your ocean blues and your earth tone tans and browns."

"But what about this one?" The BFW pulled a large gray dress out of the pile. "This is one of my favorites."

"Well, yes, that's a good one for you," I said.

"But it's not really earthy," she said.

"No, but it's, er . . . elephantine," I said. "Which is very close to earthy."

The BFW scowled.

"Why don't you try it on," I said, pulling the purple one out of her pile. "Meanwhile, I'll take this one back out."

"But do I really want to wear something that's elephantine?" the BFW asked.

"It's elephantine only in the best sense of the word," I assured her. Then, holding the purple dress up high like a shield, I left the dressing room.

If Stacy saw anything, it was only a large,

bright purple dress coming out of the dressing room next to the one I was supposed to be in. Using it as camouflage, I carried it to the front of the store, then left it on a rack and slipped outside.

"Jake?" A familiar voice called to me. I turned and saw myself jogging down the sidewalk. A second later my sister, in my body, stopped in front of me.

"What were you doing in there?" Jessica pointed my finger at the window of Scarcely Hers.

"Stacy grabbed me," I explained. "She didn't think I was dressed right for your date with Dan."

"Hmmm, I didn't think of that." Jessica tugged on my earlobe. "She's right."

We started down the sidewalk. "Forget it," I said. "I'm not going back in there. The Girl Rays'll get me."

"Girl Rays?" Jessica scowled. "What are you talking about?"

"I'm talking about not turning into any more of a girl than I already am," I said. "There is no way I'm wearing a short skirt or a see-through blouse. Just forget it. It's out of the question."

"I'm not saying you have to wear a see-through blouse," said my sister in my body. "But if you don't look nice, Dan's just going to get more interested in Sumi."

"Wait a minute." I stopped outside Vinny's Pizzeria and turned to her. "I thought you said Dan was only interested in Sumi as a friend."

"Well, I *hope* that's the case." Jessica bit my lip.

"It better be . . . " I didn't finish the sentence because of what I saw through the window of Vinny's. Inside, Dan and Sumi were sitting at the counter.

And Dan had his arm around her shoulder again!

28

"You see what I see?" I asked.

Jessica, in my body, stared through the window. "Why that — !" She yanked open the pizzeria door and I followed her in.

Inside, Dan had his arm around Sumi's shoulder while he showed her how to fold a slice of pizza the long way.

"See," he was saying. "You fold it like this so you can hold the crust. Then you start eating at the point."

My sister and I watched as Dan helped Sumi guide the folded slice of pizza toward her mouth. Sumi giggled. Jessica, in my body, clenched and unclenched my fists.

"Ahem!" She cleared my throat loudly.

Dandy Dan looked over his shoulder. "What do you want, Jake?" Then he noticed me in my sister's body. His arm slid away from Sumi's shoulder. "Oh, uh, hi, Jessica, what are you doing here?"

"We thought you were going to wait for us back at school," said my sister in my body.

"I was, but Sumi said she was hungry," Dan explained.

"It's not his fault," Sumi said. "I was very hungry after that long trip. And I have always wanted to try American pizza."

"So how do you like it?" I asked.

Sumi smiled. "It really rots, Jessica."

My sister, in my body, turned to me. "Know what, Jessica? I think we should take Sumi home and show her an American house. I bet she'd really like that."

"Good idea," Dan said.

Jessica made a frown appear on my face. I could see she wasn't happy with the idea of Dan coming to our house with Sumi. She proceeded to twist my face into all sorts of strange looks. I got the message.

"Uh, I think it would be better if you didn't come," I said.

"Why not, Jessica?" Dan asked me.

"Uh . . . " Stuck for a reason, I glanced at my sister in my body. She mouthed something. It seemed like she was saying, "The door."

"The door," I said to Dan.

"The door?" He scowled. "Yeah, so?"

I glanced back at my sister, who was shaking my head furiously. Once again she mouthed some words.

"Oh!" Now I understood and turned to Dan. "I meant, the *dog*."

"What about it?" Dan asked.

Good question. I looked to my sister again. She bared my teeth, opened my mouth and snapped it shut.

"He bites," I said.

"Oh." Dan's pimply forehead creased. "Then, do you really think Sumi should go?"

"He doesn't bite girls," I said.

Dan turned to my sister in my body. "What about you, Jake? Does he bite you?"

"Oh, he wouldn't bite me," Jessica, in my body, replied. "But that's because I've known him since he was a puppy."

I could have added that Lance only bites guys with acne problems, but I knew my sister would kill me.

"Well, okay, I better not go." Dan looked disappointed, but then he brightened. "But I'll see you guys at the carnival in a little while, right?"

Jessica shook my head violently. It appeared that she didn't want to go to the carnival after all.

"Well, maybe the carnival isn't such a good idea," I said.

Dan frowned. Behind him, Jessica again shook my head. I didn't understand what she was trying to say.

"Uh, could you excuse us for a moment?" Jessica, in my body, said to Dan. Then she took me by the arm and led me out the door.

"Now what?" I sputtered when we got out to the sidewalk.

"Tell him Sumi and I aren't going," she hissed. "You'll go with him."

"Me go to the carnival alone with Zitface?" I shook my sister's head emphatically. "Dream on, Jessica."

"Did you see him with that pizza?" Jessica, in my body, asked heatedly. "He was all over her!"

"I thought he was just being 'friendly,'" I reminded her.

Jessica narrowed my eyes at me. "Okay, maybe I was wrong. Maybe he really does like her. But you can't blame him. Sumi happens to be incredibly beautiful. *Any* boy would be attracted to her."

"Why do you keep making excuses for him?" I asked. "Face it, Jess, the guy's pure slime. He'd probably put the moves on an amoeba if it was the only living thing around."

My sister ignored me. "Sumi's leaving with her father tonight. I'm sure that as soon as she's gone he'll forget about her."

"You're right," I said. "He forgets about *every* girl as soon as they're out of his sight."

Jessica grit my teeth and started tugging on my earlobe again.

"Stop doing that!" I said.

My sister stopped tugging. "Jake, please, I was really looking forward to going to the carnival with him this afternoon. Now I'm stuck in your body, and you're in mine, please tell him you'll go."

"Forget it, Jess. He'll probably put his arm around my shoulder and try to show *me* how to eat pizza."

Jessica sighed with disappointment and made my shoulders sag. "All right. We'll tell him we've made other plans for Sumi this afternoon. I may not get to be with him, but at least he won't be with her."

Just then the door to Vinny's Pizzeria swung open and Sumi and Dan came out.

"Jessica and Jake," Sumi said. "Would you mind if Dan took me to the carnival for a little while? I know I'm here to visit you, but I've always wanted to go to an American carnival. I promise I won't be long."

I watched Jessica, in my body, scramble for an answer. "On second thought, Sumi," she said. "Why don't you go to the carnival with Dan and Jessica?"

29

Dan said he'd meet us at the entrance to the carnival. Sumi, Jessica, and I went back to our house and had iced tea in the kitchen. Then my sister, in my body, shoved my hands into my pockets and turned to me. "Well, Jessica, I guess you ought to go change."

I gave her a funny look. She knew I couldn't change until tonight when we went back to school. Until then I was stuck in her body.

My sister tugged on my earlobe and added, *"Clothes."*

"Oh." Now I understood.

"Maybe we all ought to go up to your room," she suggested.

"Sure." I led the way up the stairs and into my room. Sumi glanced around at the sports posters on the walls and the video games with a puzzled expression. "This is *your* room, Jessica?"

Ooops! "Actually, this is Jake's room," I said. "I just thought you might like to see it."

We went across the hall to Jessica's bedroom. Inside, Sumi looked around in wonder.

"It's so big!" she gasped.

"Not really," replied my sister, in my body.

"Oh, yes, Jake, it is," Sumi said. "Compared to my room at home it is very big. In Tokyo we have so many people and so little space. My room is half this size. And look — " she turned to me and pointed at my sister's telephone — "you have your own phone."

"I have to," I said. "Otherwise, no one else in the family would ever get to make a call."

"Why, Jessica?" Sumi asked.

"Because I get so many phone calls," I said.

"You must be a very popular girl," Sumi said.

"Oh, yes, I am extremely popular," I said. "I am the most popular girl in the tenth grade. In fact, I am probably one of the most popular girls in the world. I am — "

"Uh, Jessica," my sister, in my body, interrupted. "I think you're bragging."

"Oh, no, I'm not bragging," I said, still pretending to be her. "I'm simply stating a true fact."

"I think it's time to change your clothes." Jessica, in my body, went into her closet and started to look for things for me to wear.

"Do you like my hair, Sumi?" I asked, running my sister's fingers through her kinky reddish hair. "It used to be straight and brown, but I had it curled up. I also added the reddish color."

"It's, uh, very nice," Sumi said uncertainly.

"Actually, I think it's as ugly as dried seaweed," I said. "I only did it because I thought Zitface would like it."

"Zitface?" Sumi frowned. "Who is Zitface?"

"Oh, uh, that's what I call Dan," I said. "Zitface means he's got — "

"A very nice face," my sister, in my body, interrupted again. "It's just a saying kids around here use. It probably hasn't gotten to Japan yet."

"Like rots," Sumi observed.

"Uh . . . exactly," my sister said uncertainly.

"So you could say Zitface's looks really rot?" Sumi asked.

"Definitely," I agreed.

My sister, in my body, glowered at me. By then she'd pulled out a bunch of her clothes for me to wear. She dumped them on her bed. "Why don't you try these on, Jessica?"

Sumi made a funny face but said nothing. I started to pull off the baggy sweatshirt, but then stopped. My sister, in my body, was standing with my arms crossed, watching and waiting.

"Would you mind?" I said.

"Would I mind what?"

I put my sister's hand on her hip and struck a pose. "Can't a girl get some privacy around here?"

Jessica rolled my eyes so hard I was afraid

they were going to come loose in my head. She stomped out of the room, banging the door closed behind her.

I started to try on the clothes she'd taken out of the closet. I didn't care if Sumi watched. After all, she was a girl and I was a girl, at least until tonight.

"Does your brother always pick your clothes for you?" Sumi asked as I tried on a white turtle-neck with a red plaid skirt.

"Uh . . . oh, yes," I replied. "Jake has wonderful taste."

"He is also a very good football player," Sumi said.

"Yes," I said. "As you've probably noticed, Jake is an incredible, multi-gifted and talented person."

"You must really love your brother," Sumi observed.

"*Everyone* loves Jake," I said. "Girls call here all the time. To tell you the truth, Sumi, you were very lucky he had time to see you today. He had to break several dates."

"But I still don't understand why he lied about his age," Sumi said.

"Oh, well, can I tell you a secret?" I asked.

Sumi nodded.

"I think in some ways Jake is very frustrated," I said. "You see, he's so much smarter and more mature than the other boys in his grade. He only lied about his age because he needs to find people on his own level."

"But he does have friends his age," Sumi pointed out. "Those two boys, Josh and Andy."

"He makes an exception for them," I said. By then I'd tried on a bunch of Jessica's outfits. I decided to go back to the white turtleneck and plaid skirt.

Rap! Rap! There was a knock on the door.

"Yes?" I said.

"Are you *decent?*" my sister filled my voice with sarcasm.

"Yes, Jake, you can come back in now."

My sister, in my body, came back into the room. When she saw the outfit I'd selected, she nodded my head. "Okay, that's a start."

Something about the way she said that made me nervous. "A start?" I repeated. "What does that mean?"

Jessica, in my body, smiled. "Now we have to do your face."

30

I swallowed. "My face?"

My sister put one of my hands on my hip and bent the other in a very un-guylike way. "Well, of course, silly. You didn't think someone as *popular* as you could go on a date *without makeup*, did you?"

"Uh . . . " I glanced at Sumi and realized that I couldn't say out loud what I was thinking. But this was bad. I may have been in a girl's body, but the idea of wearing makeup was still totally gross.

"Let's see, now . . . " In my body, my sister pressed one of my fingers against my lip. "What shall we do with you?"

I noticed that Sumi was watching my sister in my body carefully. Jessica wasn't helping things by pretending to act like such a . . . a weirdo. She started to guide me across the room.

"Wh . . . where are we going, Jake?" I asked nervously.

"To your makeup table, Jessica, where else?"

I hesitated. "Come to think of it, Jake, I think I'd prefer the natural look today."

"Oh, really?" my sister raised my eyebrows skeptically. "Is that why you had your hair permed and highlighted?"

"Uh . . . " I swallowed. She had me on that one.

"Now come on." She tugged me toward the makeup table. "The natural look is totally lame, Jessica. I'm not going to let you leave this room until you look gorgeous."

With Sumi there I couldn't really argue. Jessica, in my body, led me to the makeup table and made me sit down. I looked into the mirror. What I saw was very strange — me, in my sister's body. Meanwhile, standing behind me was my sister in my body. She had a devilish look on my face. I knew I was in big trouble.

"The important thing is to make you look really great for Dan," she said. "This definitely calls for false eyelashes."

"Wha . . . " I gasped.

"Now, now, Jessica," she said. "Don't be modest. You know how fabulous you look in them."

Half an hour later she was finished. I looked into the mirror and studied my, I mean, my sister's face. It looked like a mask. The skin was powdered. The cheeks were darkened with reddish-brown blush. False eyelashes were glued to the eyelids, which were also blackened with mascara. Eyeliner and eye shadow had also been added. My sister's lips were one shade of red, and their outline, another, darker shade.

As I stared at the face looking back at me I almost felt sorry for girls. I mean, the idea that they go through all this junk in an effort to look good. Covering their faces with sticky, slimy paints. Gluing fake stuff on. Burning their hair with chemicals to make it curly and to change the colors. . . .

Meanwhile, all a guy had to do was take a shower, put on clean clothes, and comb his hair.

My sister, in my body, and Sumi appeared in the mirror behind me.

"So what do you think?" Jessica asked.

"You have done a beautiful job, Jake," Sumi praised her.

I watched as my sister made a smile appear on my face. She dusted my hands together proudly. "Piece of cake."

"Is it common for brothers to make up their sisters here?" Sumi asked.

"Not really," my sister, in my body, replied. "It's just something I've always been naturally good at."

"Oh, I see." Sumi sounded a little uncertain.

"Like I said before, my brother is really unusual," I quickly added. "It's very rare for a boy his age to feel so confident about his masculinity that he doesn't mind helping me with my makeup. He wouldn't have to do it if I weren't such a bonehead about these things. I'm very lucky to have a brother like Jake."

In the mirror my sister, in my body, narrowed my eyes angrily. "A bonehead, huh?"

"Yes." I nodded her head. "I'm just totally helpless when it comes to makeup. I'd be lost without Jake."

My sister, in my body, rubbed my jaw pensively. "Hmmm, that reminds me, I almost forgot the patchouli oil."

31

"No!" I launched my sister's body out of the chair and away from the makeup table. "There's no way. Forget it! I'm not wearing that stuff!"

Jessica, in my body, pretended to look puzzled. In my hand she held the vial of the smelly oil. "But you *always* wear it, Jess."

"Uh, not today. I've changed my mind."

"What is it?" Sumi asked.

Jessica, in my body, opened the vial and held it out.

Sumi took a sniff. "That smells very interesting."

"Well, I'm not interested in smelling *interesting*," I said.

"But it makes you unique," my sister, in my body, said. "The other girls all wear the same old perfumes. This makes you distinctive."

"I think you mean, di-*stink*-tive," I replied. "With the emphasis on *stink*."

My sister put my hands on my hips and shook my head in disappointment. "I really don't understand you, Jessica. One moment you're raving about what a brilliant makeup artist I am and how you'd be helpless without me. The next moment you're refusing my best fashion advice."

"In this one case you're wrong," I said.

"But how would a *bonehead* like you know?" my sister, in my body, asked.

"A girl's got a right to her own opinion," I replied and crossed my sister's arms firmly.

Jessica, in my body, turned to Sumi. "Can you believe how ungrateful he, er . . . I mean, *she* is?"

Not wanting to let my sister get away with that, I also turned to Sumi. "Don't let her, er . . . I mean, *him* drag you into this, Sumi. This is between me and my sis — I mean, brother."

Sumi's forehead creased. She tapped her wristwatch with her finger. "I think we better go. Dan will be waiting for us at the carnival."

She was right. I turned to my sister in my body. "Ready?"

"Uh . . . " My sister hesitated and then glanced at our guest. "Would you mind waiting outside for a second, Sumi? I want to speak to my, er . . . sister for a moment in private."

"Okay." Sumi left the room. Jessica, in my body, went to the door and closed it. Then she turned to me.

"I want you to stick to Dan like glue," she said.

"Don't let him get any time alone with Sumi."

"Well, with you and I both there, that shouldn't be a problem," I said.

"You don't get it, Jake," my sister said. "I'm not going with you."

"What are you talking about? Of course, you're going."

"No way," she said. "I don't want my geeky brother going along on my dates."

"Are you serious?" I gasped.

"Believe it," she said.

"I have to handle Dan alone?" What a horrible thought!

"Yes, and *stop biting my nails*!"

I wasn't even aware that I was doing it. I pulled my sister's fingers away from her mouth. "You can't do this to me. I can't do it alone. If you don't go, I don't go."

Jessica pointed my finger at me. "If *you* don't go, he's going to be alone with Sumi the whole time."

Uh-oh. I didn't like that either. I wanted to be with Sumi. And if I couldn't be with her in *my* body, being with her in my sister's body was the next best thing. But the only way I could do that was by going to the carnival. "Why can't you come?"

"I told you. I don't want my geeky brother coming along on my dates."

"Just this one time?" I asked.

Jessica shook my head. "No, it sets a bad precedent."

"Look, we'll make an exception," I begged. "You come along on this date and I *promise* that after we get our own bodies back I'll never want to come along on a date with you."

"What about to a concert?" she asked.

"I promise I won't ask to go," I said.

"A movie?"

"If I really want to see it, I'll go with my friends," I said.

"Suppose a boy I know gets tickets to a football game?" my sister asked.

"Uh . . . " I hesitated. "You mean, a *pro* game?"

Jessica nodded my head.

"That's sports," I said.

"So? I would still be on a date," she said.

"But you're talking about a *pro* football game," I said. "In a *real* stadium with hot dogs and soda and TV coverage. How could you go and not take me? That would be totally unfair. Date or no date, it's against the rules. Come on, Jessica, blood is thicker than water. You couldn't leave me behind."

Jessica let out a big sigh. "You're really pathetic, Jake."

32

Jessica, in my body, finally agreed to go to the carnival. But not with Dan, Sumi, and me. Since she was in my body, she would go with my friends, Josh and Andy.

Even Sumi argued that she should go with us, but Jessica, in my body, insisted that it was better if she went with my friends. Since Josh lived on the way to the carnival, Jessica, Sumi, and I walked there together.

Andy and Josh were waiting for us outside Josh's house. They both grinned when they saw me, in my sister's body, all dressed up.

"Oh, Jessica, I just *adore* your makeup," Andy gushed.

"And that's the *cutest* little outfit!" added Josh.

"I'm sure Dan's going to love you in it!" Andy said.

"Very funny," I grumbled. If I hadn't been in my sister's body I would have slugged them both.

We headed for the carnival. From a block away we could see the Ferris wheel and hear the joyful shouts and squeals of kids on the rides. As we got closer, the sounds of the crowd grew louder, mixed with the clanging of bells and the hiss of helium balloons. Now we could see the booths where you could knock down lead bottles or sink baskets for prizes.

Dan was waiting for us at the entrance to the carnival. When he saw Sumi and me, he smiled broadly and walked toward us. I stopped and cringed at the thought of him hugging me.

But he walked right past me in my sister's body.

And stopped in front of Sumi.

"Glad you could make it," he said. "Ready?"

"Yes." Sumi nodded eagerly.

The next thing I knew, Dan took her hand and led her in.

An elbow poked me in the ribs. It was from my sister in my body. "Don't just stand there," she whispered. "Go with them!"

I hurried to catch up with Dan and Sumi.

"Don't they have carnivals in Japan?" Dan was asking her.

"Not like this," Sumi replied, looking around wide-eyed at the game booths filled with stuffed animals and other prizes, and at the vendors selling T-shirts and balloons you could put your own photograph on.

"Hey, cutie!" a carny with long scraggly hair waved at her. He was standing inside a booth with a counter lined with water rifles. On the opposite wall was a row of plastic clowns' faces with open mouths.

Sumi stopped. The wall beside the carny was lined with pink-and-blue stuffed animals of all sizes.

"Want the big bunny?" the carny yelled, pointing at one really big pink bunny.

Sumi nodded eagerly.

"Then step up and try your luck." The carny grinned, revealing a big gap in his front teeth. "It's only a dollar a try."

Sumi gave Dan a questioning look. The carny caught on quick.

"Come on, sport," he yelled at Dan. "Give your girlfriend a buck. Don't you want to get a bunny for your honey? It's only a buck."

Dan slid his hands into his pockets and glanced at me out of the corner of his eye. "Hey, Jessica, I'm a little short on cash. Think you could help Sumi out?"

How could I refuse? Sumi was our guest. I took a dollar out of my sister's wallet and gave it to the carny. By now some other people had come along and they also paid.

"Everyone pick up a water rifle," the carny said. "The first one to make their balloon pop wins the prize."

The others picked up their rifles, but Sumi looked uncertainly at hers.

"Ever shot a rifle before, honey?" the carny asked.

Sumi shook her head.

The carny turned to Dan. "Go on, sport, give her a hand."

The next thing I knew, Dan stepped up behind Sumi and helped her pick up the rifle and aim it. His arms went around her and his lips were next to her ear as he whispered instructions. *And I was paying for him to do that!*

A bell rang and everyone shot a thin spray of water out of their rifles and into the clowns' mouths. Balloons began to rise out of the clowns' heads.

Pop! Sumi's balloon exploded. Her jaw dropped and her eyes widened with surprise. She looked like she thought she'd done something wrong.

"Cutie's a winner!" the carny cried, handing her a little stuffed bunny.

The expression on Sumi's face went from worry to delight to puzzlement.

"Hey," Dan said to the carny. "I thought you said she'd win the big bunny."

"Not on the first try, buster," replied the carny. "You gotta win again to get the big bunny."

Sumi turned to Dan and gave him a doe-eyed

look. You could see how much she wanted to win the big bunny. But that meant paying more money. Dan turned to me in my sister's body. "You don't want to disappoint your guest, do you, Jessica?"

33

It turned out that winning a second time didn't earn the big bunny either. Instead it earned a bunny that was just a little larger than the first one.

Eleven games later, Sumi was still shooting.

Dan didn't have his hand around her shoulders anymore.

Now it was around her waist.

"What's going on?" someone whispered behind me.

I looked back and found my sister, in my body, along with Josh and Andy. "Sumi's trying to win a big stuffed bunny," I whispered back.

"Why does Dan have his arm around her?" Jessica asked.

"He must think she needs support," I said.

"Hey, Jessica?" Dan turned to me. "Think I could have some more money? Sumi's getting real close to winning the big bunny."

"Uh, sure." I took out my sister's wallet and gave him another dollar.

"How long has this been going on?" my sister, in my body, gasped.

"Uh, so far it's cost you about twelve bucks," I replied.

"*What!?*"

"Well, Sumi *really* wants that bunny," I tried to explain.

The next thing I knew, my sister, in my body, was dragging me away from the booth. Dan and Sumi didn't even notice because they were totally involved in the game.

"Do you know what you're doing?" Jessica was acting really agitated. "You're using *my money* to pay for Dan to put his arm around Sumi!"

"What else am I supposed to do?" I asked.

"Don't give him any more money," Jessica said.

"Then Sumi won't get her bunny," I said.

Jessica rolled my eyes. "Tough noogies."

"Oh, yeah?" I said. "*You* tell Sumi she can't have her bunny."

Jessica, in my body, muttered something unrepeatable.

"Hey, watch your mouth," I warned her.

"It's not *my* mouth, it's *your* mouth," my sister, in my body, reminded me. "And I can make it say anything I like."

"Why you . . . " I started to make a fist with my sister's hand.

But then I felt a tap on my shoulder. "Jessica?"

I turned and found Dan behind me. Sumi was still shooting the water rifle. "Yes, Dan?" I asked.

"Listen, Sumi has to leave with her father in a little while." Dan said in a low voice so Sumi wouldn't hear. "I think it would be nice if we all got together and gave her a going away present. Something she can remember us by."

I glanced over at my sister, in my body, who sort of shrugged and nodded. It sounded like an okay idea.

Dan told us how much money he thought it would cost. Of course, he was "a little short of cash" again, so Jessica, in my body, and I, in hers, coughed up the money.

Dan pocketed the money. "Tell Sumi I'll be right back."

Dandy Dan disappeared into the crowd while we waited for Sumi to finish the game. She still hadn't popped enough balloons to win the big bunny, but the carny gave her a medium-size one.

"Nice going," I congratulated her.

Sumi smiled crookedly. "I wanted to win the big one, but I think he would have made me play all night."

"Hey, don't worry," I said, thinking about the gift Dan was going to give her from all of us. "I bet you'll get something *really* nice before long."

34

I can't say I had a great time at the carnival after Dan rejoined us. Even though Jessica had worked really hard to make me look good in her body, Dan hardly paid any attention to me. I guess I should have been relieved that he chose to put his arm around Sumi's waist and not mine, but after a while I actually started to feel a little jealous. It wasn't right for him to ignore me, I mean Jessica.

I mean, after all, my sister was the person he'd originally asked to the carnival. Sumi was just a last minute add-on.

But now I was the one who felt like the add-on, sitting behind those two on the roller coaster while Dan had his arm around Sumi's shoulder (of course!) and they both screamed with fear and delight.

And it was the same with the rest of the rides and games. Dan acted like I wasn't even there.

Finally it was time to go. We met up with

Andy, Josh, and my sister in my body, and left the carnival together. Sumi was flushed with delight and excitement as we walked home. She was so happy that it was hard not to feel good for her.

"This was the best day!" she said. "Thank you so much!"

Josh and Andy said they had to go home. Jessica and I both reminded Josh that we'd see him at Mr. Dirksen's science lab during the choir performance that night.

"So, uh, what're your plans for the rest of the day, sweetie?" Andy asked me with a wink.

"I think I'll hide," I grumbled.

Sumi, Dan, Jessica, in my body, and I walked the rest of the way to my house. A car was parked at the curb. I had a feeling it must have been the one Sumi's father had rented.

We were going up the front walk when the door opened and my father and Mr. Hoshino came out.

"Perfect timing," Dad said. "We were just going to look for you. Mr. Hoshino and Sumi have to go to the airport and catch a plane."

Dad walked with Mr. Hoshino down to the car. Sumi turned to Jessica, in my body. "Well, Jake, I guess I have to say good-bye. I hope we will still be pen pals."

"You can bet on it," my sister, in my body, replied.

Sumi turned to me, in my sister's body, next.

"It was very nice to meet you, Jessica."

"You too, Sumi." I shook her hand.

Finally, Sumi turned to Dan. "Thank you for making my day so much fun."

"It was my pleasure," Dan said. "And we bought you a little gift to remember us by." He opened a bag he was carrying and pulled out a white T-shirt.

"Oh, you shouldn't have!" Sumi cried and clasped her hands together happily.

I felt my sister's mouth fall open in shock. On the front of the T-shirt was a big photograph of . . . Dan's face!

That was how Sumi was supposed to remember us!?

"Sumi!" Mr. Hoshino called from the car. "Come on, we have to go!"

"I'm coming!" Sumi called back. Then she threw her arms around Dan's neck. "Thank you so much! This really rots, you zitface!"

35

Jessica, in my body, and I had the same exact reaction. We both clamped our hands over our mouths to keep from bursting out in laughter. By the time Dan recovered from his shock, Sumi was in the car and waving out the window at us.

Mr. Hoshino's car went down the street, turned the corner, and disappeared. Dan turned to us with his mouth agape and a shocked look on his face.

"Did you hear *that*?" he sputtered. "She said my present rotted and called me a zitface! Is that any way to show gratitude?"

My sister and I shared a look. Somehow we didn't feel the least bit sorry for him.

"After all I did for her . . . " Dan puffed out his chest and straightened up. "Well, she'll see. If she ever comes back here, forget it, I won't give her the time of day. That babe is history."

Jessica, in my body, and I listened in amazement. Who did he think he was? The world's greatest stud?

Now Dan turned to me. "So, Jessica, what do you feel like doing tonight?"

I couldn't believe it! He'd just spent the whole afternoon ignoring me, I mean Jessica, and now he wanted to do something?

My sister's stomach rumbled hungrily. "I think I'm going to go inside and get something to eat," I said.

"Me too," said Jessica, in my body.

"Good idea," said Dan. "I'm pretty hungry myself."

Jessica, in my body, and I, in hers, shared a look. I led the way up the walk and in the front door. Jessica, in my body, followed, and Dan brought up the rear.

Only, as soon as Jessica got inside, she slammed the door shut.

Rap! Rap! Dandy Dan knocked on the door. "Hey, open up! Hey, Jake, how come you shut the door on me? Open up!"

Inside my sister and I smiled and gave each other a high five.

As far as we were concerned, Dandy Dan was history.

36

We still had a few hours to kill until the choir performed. I was feeling sort of tired so I decided to take a nap in Jessica's room.

Later I woke up, got out of bed, and dragged myself over to my sister's makeup table. What I saw in the mirror was gruesome. My sister's hair was a mess. Her makeup was smeared, her eyes were puffy, and her clothes were wrinkled.

I really looked horrible. I knew it would take hours before I'd look good again. This was too much pressure after a long, hard day. I felt the tears start to roll down my sister's cheeks. I just couldn't deal with it.

Rap! Rap! "Jake?" Jessica knocked on the door.

"Yeah?" I lifted my sister's head and looked in the mirror again. Now her eyes were red and watery.

"Are you okay?" Jessica asked through the door.

"No." I sniffed.

The door opened and my sister, in my body, came in. She was still wearing my clothes. But she'd brushed my hair and washed my face. Somehow, *she* looked fine. "What's the matter?"

"I just can't take it," I sobbed. "The makeup, the hair, the clothes — it's too much!"

"Now, now, it's not *that* bad." Jessica patted me, in her body, on the shoulder. "I'll help you through it. Go wash your face. You'll feel better."

I went into the bathroom and washed my sister's face. After that I felt a little better. Jessica, in my body, was waiting in her room. She was ready to go to school.

"I can't believe how easy it is for you," I moaned.

"Don't worry," she said. "You only had to go through it *today*. In an hour you'll be back in your own body. How would you like to face clothes, makeup, and hair *every morning* for the rest of your life?"

"Forget it." I shook her head. "Not a chance."

37

Josh was waiting outside the main entrance of school when Jessica and I got there. A lot of kids and their parents were going in to hear the choir.

"Ready to switch back?" he asked.

Jessica nodded my head and I nodded hers.

"Okay, let's go." We went into school.

"*Hey, wait!*" Andy jogged toward us carrying something orange in his hand. As he got closer I realized they were day lilies, which grew wild along the road. He must have picked a few on his way to school.

"Here, Jessica." Gasping for breath, he held the flowers out to me.

"What's this for?" I asked.

"Well, uh, I was wondering if you'd be my valentine," he said with a grin.

I rolled my sister's eyes. "Very funny, dork-brain."

"Aw, come on," Andy begged.

"Get real, weirdo," I said.

"But don't you see?" he said. "If you say yes, then after you and Jessica switch back, she still has to be my valentine."

I turned to my sister in my body and saw a look of horror come over my face. "Jake, please, don't!" she begged.

I had to admit it was a funny idea.

But I shook my sister's head. "Sorry, Andy. Jessica's already been through enough."

Andy's shoulders sagged with disappointment. "Darn," he muttered. "Some friend."

"Come on, we better do this before Principal Blanco notices us," Josh said.

We went into school and hurried down to Mr. Dirksen's science lab. Jessica turned on the lights, and we quickly got into our seats while Josh hunched over the keyboard.

"Ready?" he called out.

"Ready!" my sister and I both replied.

"Here goes!" Josh pressed the red button.

Whump!

38

Amazingly, the switch back to our own bodies went perfectly. I checked all over and was a hundred-percent Jake.

"Oh, wow!" Jessica gasped, looking at her arms and then feeling her face with her fingers. "I'm me again!"

"And no worse for the wear," I added.

During the switch, Andy had been over by the animal tanks. Now he came back with some small creatures in his hands. "Hey, guys, want to have some fun? Let's switch a toad with a mouse."

"That's ridiculous," Josh said.

"Aw, come on," Andy said, putting the toad down on one of the chairs and the mouse on the other. "It'll be cool."

"Forget it," Josh said. "I'm out of here before Principal Blanco catches us."

Just then the door opened.

Principal Blanco stepped in.

He scanned the room. Jessica was nowhere in sight. She must've ducked behind one of the lab tables.

"You boys can't stay out of here, can you?" the principal said.

"Uh, we only came in to do some extra credit work," Josh quickly said.

"On a Saturday night?" Principal Blanco scowled.

"We figured it was a good way to stay out of trouble," Andy said.

"Well, you just found yourself in a different kind of trouble," our principal said. Then he paused and sniffed. "Wait a minute. I smell something." He looked at me. "It's that stuff your sister wears, Jake. If she's in this room again she's going to be in big, big trouble. I was serious about that month of detention."

Principal Blanco started to look around. I knew it wouldn't take him long to find Jessica. It wasn't fair. After everything Jessica and I had been through, I really didn't want her to get a month's detention.

Meanwhile, Principal Blanco stopped at one of the chairs attached to the DITS. "What's this mouse doing here?"

It was the mouse Andy had left on the second chair. Meanwhile, the toad was still sitting on the first chair. Our principal bent over the second chair to look at the mouse.

Suddenly, I had an idea. I reached over to the computer console and pressed the red button. At that moment, the mouse jumped off the chair and scurried away across the floor.

Whump!

39

When the haze cleared, Principal Blanco was squatting on the floor with his hands between his knees. He blinked and puffed out his cheeks with air.

Over on the first chair, a small toad was croaking like crazy.

Josh turned to me. He looked pale. "Do you realize what you just did, Jake?"

"It's only temporary," I said, looking over at the lab tables. "Hey, Jessica, you can come out."

Jessica stood up. "What happened?"

"Principal Blanco had a slight accident," I said. "You better bail before he figures it out."

Jessica hurried toward the door. "Thanks, Jake, I owe you one."

A second later, she was gone.

I quickly pressed the red button again.

Whump!

The room filled with haze. When it cleared, Principal Blanco was standing near the second chair with a dazed expression on his face. He blinked and shook his head as if he was trying to clear it. "What happened?"

"What do you mean?" I asked innocently.

"Something very strange just happened," the principal said. "You must have noticed."

I turned to Josh and Andy. "Do you guys know what he's talking about?"

They shook their heads.

"It was bizarre," Principal Blanco said. "For a moment I could have sworn I was a toad. Can you imagine that?"

All too easily, I thought, trying not to smile.

About the Author

Todd Strasser has written many award-winning novels for young and teenage readers. Among his best-known books are *Help! I'm Trapped in Obedience School* and *Abe Lincoln for Class President.* He speaks frequently at schools about the craft of writing and conducts writing workshops for young people. He and his family live outside New York City with their yellow Labrador retriever, Mac. His next project for Scholastic will be a series about *Camp Run-A-Muck.*